YOU
BRING
THE
DISTANT
NEAR

YOU BRING THE DISTANT NEAR

mitali perkins

FARRAR STRAUS GIROUX · NEW YORK

Farrar Straus Giroux Books for Young Readers
An imprint of Macmillan Publishing Group, LLC
175 Fifth Avenue, New York, NY 10010

fiercereads.com

Library of Congress Cataloging-in-Publication Data

Names: Perkins, Mitali, author.
Title: You bring the distant near / Mitali Perkins.
Description: First edition. | New York : Farrar Straus Giroux, 2017. |
  Summary: From 1965 through the present, an Indian American family
  adjusts to life in New York City, alternately fending off and welcoming
  challenges to their own traditions. |
Identifiers: LCCN 2016057822 (print) | LCCN 2017028520 (ebook) |
  ISBN 9780374304911 (Ebook) | ISBN 9780374304904 (hardcover)
Subjects: | CYAC: Family life—New York (State) —New York—Fiction. | East
  Indian Americans—Fiction. | Immigrants—Fiction. | New York (N.Y.)—Fiction.
Classification: LCC PZ7.P4315 (ebook) | LCC PZ7.P4315 You 2017 (print) |
  DDC [Fic]—dc23
LC record available at https://lccn.loc.gov/2016057822

Our books may be purchased in bulk for promotional, educational, or business use. Please
contact your local bookseller or the Macmillan Corporate and Premium Sales Department
at (800) 221-7945 ext. 5442 or by e-mail at MacmillanSpecialMarkets@macmillan.com.

For Jacqueline Perkins Draine,
my American mom

·CONTENTS·

FAMILY TREE

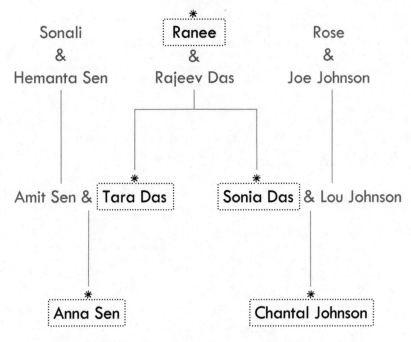

Sonali
&
Hemanta Sen

Ranee
&
Rajeev Das

Rose
&
Joe Johnson

Amit Sen & Tara Das

Sonia Das & Lou Johnson

Anna Sen

Chantal Johnson

Thou hast made me known to friends whom I knew not.
Thou hast given me seats in homes not my own.
Thou hast brought the distant near and made a brother
of the stranger. I am uneasy at heart when I have to leave
my accustomed shelter; I forgot that there abides the old
in the new, and that there also thou abidest.

—RABINDRANATH TAGORE,
from "Poems"

YOU BRING THE DISTANT NEAR

Race at the British Club

1965

THE SWIMMERS HAVE FINISHED THEIR RACES and are basking in the sun. It's almost time for the beginners' event. Tara kneels at the shallow edge, giving her little sister last-minute instructions. Floating inside her ring, Sonia pretends to listen.

Their mother stands alone by the deep end, sari-clad under the red monsoon umbrella she carries as portable shade from the West African sun. Kwasi, a Ghanaian waiter, offers her a bottle of icy cola. She refuses it. But the English mothers accept the cold drinks. Wearing starched blouses, armpits stained with sweat, they cluster in tight groups of two or three along the length of the pool. Their words melt into the sound of water lapping against children—the steamy Accra air softening even the crisp cadences of their accents. They speak briefly to Kwasi. But never to the Indian woman.

Sonia and Tara can swim at the British High Commission club only because their father works for a British company. The four Das family members are the only dark-skinned people at the club who aren't employees—something even Sonia, at age eight, can't help noticing. She feels invisible here. Sometimes she's tempted to smash a cola bottle against the cement, but she doesn't want to make more work for Kwasi. She likes how he greets her in Twi: Eti sen? *How are you?* Eh ya, she answers. *I'm fine.*

Now, with the pool water lapping against her skin, she's ready.

"Time for the youngest racers to take their marks." The British woman who's organized this day of races likes bringing order through her megaphone.

"Show them what the Das family can do, Sunny," Tara says above her.

Eight milky-skinned, freckled children bobbing in their rings take their places along the wall beside Sonia. They're all six or seven years old, but three are bigger than she is. *I'm older,* she tells herself. *I'll outsmart them.* Her toes push against the rough concrete of the pool floor. She clutches her white plastic ring under her arms, eyes fixed on the flaking blue paint on the far wall. She has to swim there and back. Fast.

Tara crouches near Sonia on the edge of the pool, silent now. The whistle blows.

"Good start, Bobby!" a mother calls.

"Go, Sunny, go!" Tara shouts.

Sonia pummels the water with her arms and pushes it behind her with her legs. Her eyes are fixed on the far wall, which is drawing closer by the second. Faster and faster she goes, churning the chlorine into the air. Redheads and towheads are falling out of her line of vision. The wall is just in front of her. All she has to do is touch it, turn, and swim back. The others are almost half a length behind her now.

She's going to win.

She's going to beat them all.

But just before she reaches the wall, she sees a tilted dome of red perched beyond it. Her mother is squatting at the edge of the pool, one arm outstretched toward the water. The hem of her sari is wet.

Sonia senses what's about to happen. She tries to slow her momentum through the water, but it's too late. Her mother catches hold of the white plastic ring and hauls it to the edge. Sonia fights, bracing her feet against the wall, but the pull is too strong. Her mother's hands grip her tightly under her arms and her body slides up, out of the pool, out of the ring.

"You've won, Baby," her mother says, throwing a towel around Sonia and pulling her into the squat of her sari.

"No! NO! *NO!*"

The other racers touch the wall, turn, and begin to bob and kick and splash back to the shallow end. Tara is running along the pavement toward her sister and mother, weaving through swimmers, waiters, and British women. None of them are watching the race in the pool. Every eye is on Sonia, who is bellowing and struggling to escape. Wildly, her fists beat against the arms and thighs that enclose her.

Tara reaches them, panting. "Ma, the race wasn't over!"

"That. Woman. Said. One. Lap," their mother answers, still wrestling to contain Sonia.

"One *lap* means there and back! She could have won!"

The winner has reached the finish line. Belatedly, the distracted crowd notices and begins to cheer.

"It is only a game, Baby," her mother says. "Be quiet."

With a howl of rage, Sonia breaks out of their mother's grasp. She flings the towel on the cement and kicks the umbrella. Then she runs to hide in the coconut trees on the far side of the pool.

"Ekhane fire ai. *Ekhunee ai.*" Her mother commands her return. *Immediately.*

Sonia doesn't obey. Ma has instructed them to use only English at the club. If she can break the rules, why can't Sonia?

All the British members are still watching them. The Das family is no longer invisible. Kwasi's is the only face that's smiling. He flashes Sonia a thumbs-up.

As if given a cue, the heavy sky suddenly empties barrels of rain over the club. In an instant, sheets of water crash on the tin roofs of the clubhouse and flood across lawns and cement. Swimmers and non-swimmers squeal, take their mothers' outstretched hands, and race through the club doors held open by Kwasi. Tara grabs the umbrella and holds it over herself and their mother as they, too, hurry to shelter.

Tara turns before they enter the clubhouse. "Come soon, Sunny!" she calls toward the coconut grove, and then she's gone.

Hair sparkling, skin gleaming, uniform drenched with rain, Kwasi takes one last look at Sonia, then disappears behind the closed doors.

Under the trees, the downpour is making the coconut fronds applaud. Sonia's sobs slowly dwindle into silence. She strides out into the rain, picks up the discarded white ring still floating at the edge of the pool, and squeezes her body back into it. The air and her skin and her swimming costume are so wet that her leap into the pool doesn't come with the usual shock. A drumbeat of Ghanaian rain keeps time as she paddles and strokes and kicks to the finish line.

1

Strangers

1973–74

Sonia

Home Is Where the Stories Are

S TARRY IS CHANNELING TWIGGY, THE BRITISH supermodel, as we board the BOAC plane in Heathrow Airport.

"We're moving to New York," she's saying to her audience at the front of the cabin. Eyes watch and ears tune in. "Father's found a fabulous post there."

I've had a front-row seat to my sister's chameleon act for years, but it still amazes me. Tara ("Starry" to me) is Indian with black hair. Twiggy is white and blond. Yet the resemblance between them is uncanny. It's more than the trendy bun, slender body, slightly Cockney accent, and clunky earrings. It's even more than the striped red, blue, and yellow dress and red tights—an exact copy of Twiggy's *Vogue* cover outfit that Ma sewed on a neighbor's borrowed machine. There's something Twiggy-ish coming from *inside* Starry that colors how she moves and talks and breathes.

"Oh, that's lovely," answers the stewardess. "You'll have to visit the theater. And the shopping on Fifth Avenue is smashing. Where are you from?"

"London," Starry responds, without hesitation.

I'm not sure I'd answer that question with just one word, like my sister. Where *are* we from? It's complicated.

Ma nudges me to enter an empty row of two seats. I settle into the one by the window and she plops down beside me. *Blimey.* I wish she'd let Starry sit there. I want to write in my diary, and my sister's presence is the next best thing to being alone. With all the packing and paperwork, privacy has been hard to find these last few weeks.

The stewardess is checking out Ma's sari and the red teep on her forehead. "But where were you *born*?" she asks my sister.

"In India," Starry answers. "But we moved to London when I was nine."

The pilot's voice crackles through the intercom, telling us that the plane is now fully boarded. Starry takes the empty seat across the aisle from Ma, and the stewardess pats her shoulder. "Well, love, we're *all* leaving London now. Fasten your seat belt, why don't you? I think the nice fellow next to you wants to help."

I lean forward. Sure enough, a young American soldier is showing my sister how to operate a seat belt—something she's known how to do since we were tiny. I have a surge of hope that Ma might tell Starry and me to switch seats. It's always safer for me to sit next to anyone male. But Ma listens for a minute to the soldier's voice; observes his gestures, medals, stripes, and uniform; and says nothing. *Oh, that's right.* If he's a "posh" young man (read: educated) raised in a "good family" (read: white or Bengali), Ma doesn't mind when Starry gets his attention. Baba always minds. He doesn't want boys around either of us, and would have taken that seat if he were here.

Ma's eyes close as the stewardesses busy themselves with preflight chores. The older-Starry-like lines of her face look tired. Maybe she'll fall asleep. If this move to New York has been exhausting, she has nobody to blame but herself. She hasn't been content anywhere we've lived. Baba faults her for making us leave India. We joined him once for a few months in Ghana, but she hated it. After that, we stayed in London while Baba traveled to Singapore, Malaysia, Cameroon, and the Philippines on short-term engineering contracts. His income wasn't steady, and landlords didn't like letting flats to "curry-cookers." So we had to shift within London three times. And our application for British citizenship kept getting denied. Baba came and went, came and went, and the fighting between them got worse. Especially when Starry started attracting men as well as boys.

While Baba was in Malaysia, a drunk neighbor banged on our door shouting, "Marry me, my Indian princess!" Baba was so upset when he heard, he wanted to move us back to Calcutta. I was furious. Calcutta?! Where my grandmothers cried because I wasn't a boy? *How can you give a strange middle-aged British man that much power over our lives?* I demanded. *I'm sorry the world is like that, Mishti,* Baba answered. *But my job is to protect you girls from those kinds of idiots.* Thankfully, for once Ma agreed with me. *I'm not moving in with your mother,* she argued. *I'll be judged right and left. No privacy. No freedom.*

It was the middle of the night—their favorite time to fight. I tossed in my bed and my sister stuffed fingers in her ears. *Find a permanent job!* Ma yelled. *Move us to America!*

And now he has.

I don't blame Ma for not wanting to return to India. She doesn't talk much about her girlhood in the village. But Baba describes his ancestral jute farm with bright eyes: coconut and mango trees, perfect for a small boy to climb; a sparkling pond full of tasty fish; lush fields, green after the monsoon. But that land was taken during the war and isn't even in India now, thanks to Partition. All we could return to is a rented, joint-family flat in the overcrowded city of Calcutta, where Ma's inability to have a son would be a constant subject of conversation for other women.

The plane begins to rumble along the tarmac, picking up speed. I glance at Ma. She's definitely asleep now. My thoughts are about to boil over. Carefully, so I don't wake her, I reach for my satchel and pull out my diary and pen. There's something about putting words on a page in private that makes me feel powerful in public. It's funny, even though I love stories so much, everything *I* write about is real. Thoughts, emotions, ideas, and beliefs. It's weird how writing them down gives them weight. Baba gifted me a new notebook just before he left for New York. It's only half full because I've been writing in small letters. Shifting the satchel to block the view in case Ma's eyes open, I turn to a blank page.

Here's to a new life in New York! A fresh start for the Das family! Maybe we'll have more money. Which means maybe Ma and Baba won't fight as much. Dig, nag, dig, nag, goes Ma, and then BOOM! Baba explodes. I don't know why she can't see him the way Starry and I do. Maybe it's because she was only eighteen when her parents married her off. Baba got to pick her out of three possible brides, but she had no choice.

The plane takes off and I watch London disappear beneath a bank of clouds. *Forever?* I wonder. After making sure Ma is still asleep, I keep writing.

It's sad that I'm not sadder to leave. I'll miss Samantha and Elsa, but they promised to write. I'll miss my visits to the library, and Starry's and my tea parties with scones, clotted cream, and cucumber sandwiches. I loved our strolls with Baba along the Thames and the times he took us to the zoo or Trafalgar Square.

I'm hoping for more solitude in the Land of the Free. To write, to read, to think. In London, I was only allowed to go to the library and the park across the street alone. I'm better off than my sister, though. Since that midnight visit from the drunken neighbor, Starry's not allowed to go outside by herself at all anymore.

I lean forward again. Now that Ma's head is drooping with sleep, the flirting across the aisle has intensified. I don't worry much about Starry—she's good at protecting herself—but I like watching her in action. I study the soldier's face: blue eyes; tan skin; nice, defined jaw. You'd think my stare would draw his gaze, but he pays no attention to me. Not with Starry laughing and chatting next to him. Growing up with a beautiful older sister is like wearing a veil. *Doesn't it bother you at all?* Elsa and Samantha used to ask. *Not really*, I answered, and left it at that. I go back to my writing.

I wish I could stay invisible in boys' eyes. Lately, the few that notice me don't focus on my face, anyway. My stupid breasts seem to be getting bigger by the month. I've been trying to make them look smaller by squashing them into bras that are two sizes too small. I support American bra-burners fighting for equal rights, but I don't think I'd have the courage to take mine off. Thank God for loose T-shirts. One day, someone special is going to look past all of this exterior stuff to see the inner me. No chameleon skin required. He'll likely be an American, but I'm hoping he'll still be a bit like my Mr. Darcy. Mysterious, reserved, kind, honorable. Those qualities last longer than a nice jawline. Although Darcy probably had that, too.

Ma stirs, so I tuck my diary back into my satchel and pull out the secondhand copy of *Pride and Prejudice* Baba gave me. Is this the ninth or the tenth time I've read it? I don't keep track. *Why keep reading the same book?* Ma always asks. *What a waste of time.* She doesn't realize how easily I can make myself at home in the Bennet family's drawing room. And how much I want to feel that way in our home.

Elizabeth's good company and the sizzle of Mr. Darcy make the eight-hour flight across the Atlantic go by in a flash. I stay in Regency England as meals are served, while Ma sleeps on, and throughout Starry's chatting and laughter. It's only when the stewardess announces that we're about to land at John F. Kennedy International Airport that I put the book away.

Our plane descends through the clouds and my new city sparkles below, dazzling in the morning light. We soar over tall spires and blocky buildings, over a wide river jeweled with boats and spanned by bridges. Then, suddenly, there she is—that famous coppery green woman, raising her torch high in the harbor.

Welcome, Sonia Das! she seems to call up to me.

Thanks, Ms. Liberty! Is that a sari you're wearing? I hope not.

She doesn't answer, but I'm almost sure she's smiling. If it's a sari, I'm almost certain there's no bra under it.

The wheels come down, and we hit the tarmac with a *ta-da!* bang and a long glide. The soldier is trying to get Starry's contact information, and my sister is sweetly but firmly refusing him. "I don't know our address yet, John," she says, pulling out a mirror to adjust her bangs and add more lipstick. John gives up, watching my sister wistfully. Poor fellow. Join the queue.

Ma wakes up with a gasp, then straightens the blue silk sari Baba bought for her in Singapore. She glances across at Starry, and then swivels to take stock of my appearance. I brace myself. Sure enough, that familiar twitch of displeasure passes across her face. It's gone in a moment, but after years of rejecting her Light & Lovely skin-bleaching cream, I know what makes her wince. The darkness of my skin.

Which idiot in history decided that lighter pigment was more attractive than having more melanin? I have no idea, but somehow he managed to infect the whole world with his stupidity—including my own mother. I just don't understand it. My skin is soft and smooth and the color reminds me of rain-drenched earth. But it's as if the darkness of it keeps

Ma from noticing my assets: curly hair, a round face that makes babies smile, deep dimples in both cheeks, big eyes that notice details other people miss.

I like my face, even if Ma doesn't. I resemble Baba, and he's got presence.

We collect our carry-on luggage. Blue-eyed Soldier tries to hug Starry goodbye. Somehow my sister manages to avoid his arms—and Ma's eyes—as we disembark. Admiration from the "right" kind of boy is okay with Ma. Physical contact, though? Absolutely forbidden by both our parents. And we need our mother to be in a good mood. Starry knows this, too. Ma's about to see Baba for the first time in six months.

After a last longing look at Starry, her ex-seatmate flashes his U.S. passport and leaves customs and immigration. It takes *us* forever with our Indian passports and visas, but finally we make it through the blur of lines, paperwork, and questions from security agents.

And there, outside the opening and closing doors, is Baba.

Arms outstretched.

Tall, robust, cheerful.

Splendid.

I barrel into the smell of pipe tobacco and the scratch of his tweed suit. "Mishti!" he calls. It feels like forever since I've heard that nickname.

Oh, how I've missed him! The Das family, reunited again!

Starry hugs him next. As he draws her close, Twiggy vanishes and she's herself again. My sister. "Star!" I hear him whisper.

That's his nickname for her—what "Tara" means in English. When I was two, I started calling her "Starry" instead of "Didi," which is what most Bengali girls call an older sister. Bengalis are famous for nicknames—we each end up with about a dozen. Only outsiders call us by our proper names. I'm "Baby" to Ma (even at fifteen), "Sunny" to Starry, but I've always been Baba's "Sweetie."

Our father is wearing his hair longer, curls brushing his collar.

"You grew sideburns!" I say.

Starry and I stick to English with our parents, each other, and everybody else. Baba and Ma, though, always use Bangla at home, and speak English only with outsiders. This time, though, Baba uses English with us.

"Like them? They're all the rage. Your Baba's become a stylish young American." He smiles. "Everyone thinks I'm a pop star."

Starry and I laugh. We're hanging on to him from either side, but even if one of his arms were available, he wouldn't touch Ma. It's not proper for a married couple to show affection in public. I can see his eyes, though, taking in the graceful lines of Ma's sari and searching her face. She gives him a small smile, and hope simmers in my heart.

Baba tells us he's borrowed a car from another Bengali family who live in the building where he's rented a flat. We head to the airport garage, towing our suitcases. "The flat's not big," he tells Ma, in Bangla, of course. "New Yorkers don't call them flats, by the way. They say 'apartment.' I've already started saving to buy a house."

"That is good news," Ma says, smiling at him for the second time in a half hour. It's a record. Starry and I exchange a quick glance to mark the significance of it.

The car's old and beat up, but roomy. The upholstery smells like fenugreek and mustard seed. In London, Baba didn't drive much, and I can tell he's still not used to it. As we leave the airport, he concentrates in silence while the three of us take in the sights: tall, dark buildings that block the sun; that same gray river I saw from above; bridges coated with rust; and dented yellow taxis racing by on either side. It looks less magical than it did from the sky. I can't see the statue at all. Will this place become familiar soon? When people ask me where I'm from, will this be my answer? *I'm a New Yorker. From Flushing, Queens.*

"Almost there," Baba says as we pull off the main road. His hands are clenched on the steering wheel and the back of his neck looks sweaty.

The car stops in front of a large brick building that looks deserted. "This will be your school, girls," Baba tells us. Starry leans across me to get a glimpse.

"You'll be able to walk here from our flat, I mean, *apartment*. And that lorry is a *truck* here. The suitcases are in the *trunk*, not the boot. You'll have to learn how to speak American."

He starts driving again. One more block and we stop in front of another building. Adults and children both are entering and exiting through the open doors. I read the sign beside the steps: QUEENS PUBLIC LIBRARY, FLUSHING BRANCH.

"This is for you, Mishti," Baba says, smiling at me in the rearview mirror. "Five blocks from our new apartment."

Libraries. How I love them. My source of stories. And solitude. Where the musty smell of books greets me like the perfume in our grandmother's embrace. My old branch was two blocks from our London flat, and I went almost daily. The librarian and I both got teary when I said goodbye. And this library is almost as close! I'll get a library card tomorrow and carry back my first installment of books. Maybe I can also find a quiet corner to write in peace.

Ma is watching the patrons come and go. "Do these people live in our neighborhood?" she asks.

"Some come by train, I suppose," Baba answers. "This is the branch for Flushing."

He starts driving again and we pass a playground full of children playing on swings and slides. I'm sitting behind Ma, so I see her profile as she surveys the scene. She's not smiling. After one long, wide-eyed stare, she turns to Baba. "Is this a dangerous neighborhood?"

"Not at all," Baba answers.

The children are laughing, shouting, running. Acting like kids in playgrounds everywhere. There's nothing dangerous in sight. It's only when I imagine how it looks to Ma that I notice what I missed with my own eyes: every child in the playground is black. Some are as dark as me, some lighter. They remind me of the kids in Ghana who used to play outside the gates of the British High Commission club.

Baba drives on, turning a corner.

"You'll have to stay inside the flat after school, girls," Ma says. "And that means both of you."

Starry glances over at me. That's been a rule for her, but not for me. Baba gives Ma a quick look, and I know he's surprised, too.

"I walked to the library by myself in London," I say.

"You can go out with your sister," Ma says, and her voice is stern. "But I can't let you wander around on your own in a place like this."

A place like *what*, exactly? "But, Ma—" I start to protest.

"Chup!" she says, with a hand in the air.

Baba catches my eye in the rearview mirror and his raised eyebrows are a warning not to argue. What in the world? I'll suffocate if I can't go out by myself. Already more restrictions than ever in the Land of the Free? *I'll find a way*, I promise the empty pages in my notebook.

Our new "home" is on the third floor of a tall, narrow building across from the playground. The apartment is made up of five hot rooms—two bedrooms, one bath, a living room, and a dining room/kitchen—that feel like the inside of a tandoori oven. But it came furnished, which means our father didn't have to buy anything. Baba's prepared his usual for dinner—fish, rice, and lentils—and stocked the fridge with necessities. He also has a few surprise purchases waiting for us. Starry squeals over a secondhand television, I get a fresh notebook, and Ma looks pleased with a new sewing machine and reams of different kinds of cloth, buttons, zippers, and other supplies.

The machine brings Ma's third smile of the day—tallied by Starry and me through another silent look.

"No uniforms in American schools," Baba says. "But take your time, Ranee. The girls have clothes from London. And maybe they can wear the salwar kameez outfits my mother sent."

"I'll sew quickly," Ma says. "They need American clothes."

Baba sighs, but decides not to battle over this. "I'll leave that to you, Ranee. School starts in three weeks."

Finally—something my mother and I agree on. I hate how the cling of a sari and the cut of a salwar showcase my curves. Even the pleated skirt and tailored blouse of my school uniform always felt awkward to me. But dungarees—I mean *jeans*—and T-shirts? They're the Land-of-the-Free outfits that America exports to the rest of the world. I wore them in London on weekends, and that's what I plan to wear on school days here. As for Starry, I doubt she'll choose jeans for her first day, but I'm 100 percent sure she's not putting on a salwar. Ma keeps her in up-to-the-minute fashion, which has always been British until now.

Starry switches on the television and makes herself

comfortable on the faded sofa. "Three weeks is plenty of time to become an American."

"Don't forget you're Bengali, too," Baba says. "Which reminds me, Star. I've hired our neighbor to keep up your harmonium lessons. And your Rabindra Sangeet."

My sister groans. "Do I have to, Baba?"

"You're a Bengali girl, aren't you? Tagore songs are a must. I'm afraid you're forgetting how to speak our beautiful language."

My sister doesn't say it aloud, but I see it clearly on her face: *So is Sunny. Why doesn't* she *have to take lessons?*

Starry's expressions are easy to read. Her Twiggy bun is gone, and Baba tugs gently on her braid. "I'm sorry, Star, but you're the one with your mother's musical talent. Hearing her sing 'Utal Dhara Badal Jhare' when we first met took my breath away."

Ma looks pleased. Starry and I have heard how our parents met before their marriage, chaperoned by our grandparents in Ma's living room. Our parents didn't speak to each other, but Ma served tea, sang that Tagore song, and—according to Baba's version—fireworks exploded and a thousand sitars burst into music.

He's right about Starry inheriting Ma's talent. My sister's paraded out at parties to make Bengali guests cry, her flute-like voice adding even more meaning to Rabindranath Tagore's songs. Even Starry has to admit the man was talented. His words can almost make you smell jasmine, hear the river splash against the side of a boat, feel a tropical breeze on your skin. Starry only performs Rabindra Sangeet when Baba asks, though. She usually sings in the shower, right before we go to bed. She loves to belt out tunes by the Beatles or the Carpenters.

Later, for her first shower in America, she chooses Simon and Garfunkel's "The Sound of Silence." I fall asleep to the familiar sound of my sister singing, and the unfamiliar sound of our parents laughing in the room next to ours.

The next morning, Baba kisses us goodbye, throws a smile in Ma's direction, and leaves for work. I try not to resent his freedom to race downstairs and stride alone to the train station. Why didn't he push back when Ma issued her new rule for us to stay inside?

"Don't worry, Sunny," Starry whispers as I watch Baba cross the street from our bedroom window. "Let her get used to life here—she'll allow you to go out alone soon."

"I'd like to visit the library," I say, my voice low. "Today, if possible."

"I'll take care of it."

It's a good thing I have Starry in my corner. We both know it's harder for Ma to say no to her than to me.

We spend the first part of the morning unpacking and cleaning. Ma makes us scrub every corner of the flat and turn the mattresses before putting on fresh sheets. "We don't know who lived here before us," she says. "I have a feeling they weren't clean people."

The rooms don't look dirty to me, and I hate that Ma is making this assumption. But I don't say anything. Instead, I scour the toilet and shower stall with energy, making sure she sees my effort.

At eleven o'clock, the three of us take a break to sip tea. I open my mouth to speak, but my sister throws me a look that clearly says, *Shut up and let me handle this.*

"Ma, how would it be if Sunny and I take a walk?" she asks, her tone sweet and polite. I do my part by placing a tin of buttery biscuits in front of our mother.

Ma sighs, takes a biscuit, and dips it into her tea. "I don't know what kind of neighborhood your father picked. The sooner we move, the better." She chews quietly, but there's a crease in her brow. "All right, then. But make sure you return in an hour."

I take time to clear away the tea before rushing to our

bedroom. My notebook is stashed beneath my socks in a drawer. Should I take it along? An hour is barely enough time to walk there, sign up for a card *and* pick out books, and then walk back. Writing is going to have to wait. I grab my empty satchel and Starry's hand and race down the stairs to freedom.

The playground is packed with kids riding bikes, playing hopscotch, and shouting at each other over the rules of different games.

"Hardly any white people in this neighborhood," Starry says. "That's why Ma doesn't like it."

"I know. I wish she wouldn't think that way."

Pulling my sister's hand, I make us pick up the pace. The streets are sizzling in the sun. London was never steamy like this, and both of us are sweating. Three boys draped across a park bench turn their heads to watch us. They're younger than me—the oldest looks about fourteen.

I let my satchel strap slip down my shoulder, hiding my rear end, but Starry's Twiggy-slim hips can't help swinging gracefully. Sweat has made her white T-shirt cling to her willowy body. My curves are hidden underneath a loose T-shirt I found at a London flea market that reads BAN BEAUTY PAGEANTS and I'm wearing an old pair of jeans one size too big for me.

A high-pitched voice calls after us. "Girlfriends? That's sooooooo sexy."

Is this child asking my sister to be his girlfriend? Starry flicks a look of contempt over her shoulder. "Try again *after* you start shaving, little man," she says, and keeps walking. I notice, though, that she drops my hand.

The other boys snicker, but that doesn't stop their friend. "Cool accent, foxy mama. But in America, chicks don't hold hands unless they're dating. *Each other,* I mean."

I turn to face him.

"Don't engage," Starry tells me in a low voice. "It's not worth it."

But I'm irritated. This child needs to be schooled. "America's a free country. Anyone can hold hands. And we are not '*chicks*,' we are human beings."

His almost-man eyes look me over, head to toe, hip to bra, and back again. "Hold mine then, my curvy queen."

"The tall one's foxier, Gerald," his friend says.

Gerald tucks a comb into his hair. "Not in my eyes. The darker the berry, the sweeter the juice."

Now I'm furious. "You foul boy. Women are not objects—"

Starry tries to pull me away. "Let's go, Sunny."

Suddenly, a fire truck pulls up right beside the playground, siren shrieking. Our three hecklers jump up and race over to where it's parking. I look around for smoke and flames, but instead of a fire, I see a grinning fireman descending from the truck carrying a big wrench and an even bigger radio. He puts the radio on the sidewalk and turns up the music. Drums start to beat and a deep, mellow voice sings, "Love and happiness, yeah, something that can make you do wrong, make you do right . . ." With two strong twists, he loosens the cap of a hydrant, releasing a shining, sunlit arc of water.

Dozens of children stream out of buildings lining the street. They're wearing swimming costumes or shorts and bare chests. Within minutes they're squealing with glee and leaping around the hydrant. They look relaxed and at home, girls and boys dancing side by side, singing along with the music. I even spot our heckler Gerald and his buddies, shirts off and jeans soaked to the skin.

Sweat is trickling down my back. I wish I could join them. We watch for a few minutes, and then make our way to the library. I take the stairs two at a time, stride through the main doors, and head for the front desk. Starry follows more slowly.

"What can I do for you?" the librarian asks. Hers is the first white face we've seen today.

"I'd like a card, please," I answer. "Sonia Das is my name."

"Oh, what a lovely accent," the librarian says, handing me a form. "Are you from England?"

I nod and start filling in the blanks on the application. Books are waiting.

"We grew up in London," my sister says, and she already sounds more American than she had on the plane. "But we're originally from India."

The librarian peers over her glasses at me and then at Starry. "Oh, are you sisters?"

"Yes, I'm seventeen, and my sister's fifteen," Starry answers. "We've just moved into the neighborhood."

I hand back my completed form. "That was fast," the librarian tells me. "Doesn't your sister want a card, too?"

"No, thanks," Starry says. "I prefer the telly—I mean television. Do you know any shows that might introduce us to life in America?"

The librarian shakes her head as she scans my application. "I don't watch much television myself. This looks fine."

She hands me a new card, and I slip it carefully into my empty satchel.

"Perhaps you've heard about a show that teenagers like?" Starry persists.

"My nieces talk quite a bit about a show called *The Brady Bunch*. It's set in a suburb of big houses, and lawns, and all—" She looks from me to Starry and back again. "Well, mostly people of European descent. I'm not sure how it will help you navigate life in Flushing, that's for sure."

"Oh, we're not staying here for long," Starry says. "We'll be moving as soon as my parents buy a house."

The librarian sighs. "That's too bad. I think you'd love it here."

"We've—"

I interrupt my sister. "Pardon me, but how many books may I check out at one time?"

"Seven. The children's room is in that direction, and we have a section for teenagers there also. Enjoy yourself, dear. And welcome to the library!"

Leaving Starry chatting with the librarian, I decide to browse the teen shelves first. *Deenie* by Judy Blume and *The Outsiders* by S. E. Hinton are both new to me, so I choose them. And then I spot an old friend—*Little Women* by Louisa May Alcott—and grab it. It's easy to become Jo March, and Laurie's another crush of mine. That's three; I can check out four more. I head to the children's shelves and find *The Secret Garden* by Frances Hodgson Burnett, *The Voyage of the Dawn Treader* by C. S. Lewis, *Hans Brinker, or The Silver Skates* by Mary Mapes Dodge, and *Heidi* by Johanna Spyri. I've been re-reading all of these for years.

"Let's go, Sunny," my sister hisses. "We've got fifteen minutes to get home. I'm sure Ma's watching the clock."

Just enough time to jog back. We pass the throng of drenched and happy children still playing in the hydrant's spray. I spot Gerald, dancing with a toddler who looks just like him. Must be his little brother. He catches sight of us but this time something feels different. Is it the books in my bag? The loud and joyful music? His hands holding his brother's? In any case, I decide to wave at him and, after one surprised look, Gerald waves back.

He and his brother were probably born here; Flushing has always been home for them. But it's going to start to feel familiar to me soon, I'm sure of it. And besides, one half of my real home is banging against my hip in my satchel. The other is in the bottom drawer of our nightstand where the pages in a notebook wait for my pen. *Where am I from?* Can the answer be stories and words, some of theirs, some of mine?

Tara

Marcia Magic

NEVER MOVE TO A SMALL APARTMENT IN Flushing, Queens, in August.

"Too bloody hot," I tell Sunny, who ignores me and opens *Little Women*.

I've been wanting to use "bloody" without earning a demerit, but now the punch of it is gone. Time for new swear words. I wonder how Americans get demerits in school.

That jog to and from the library nearly did me in, but Sunny needed her fix. She tells me I use the screen the way she uses reading and writing, but she's wrong. For her, that's escape. For me, it's research.

I fan myself with the issue of *British Pop Stars* someone

gave me as a goodbye present. It's useless to me now. Lulu, Diana, and Twiggy aren't famous enough in New York. I need to become someone new, but who? *Whom*, corrects the voice of a grammar-school teacher in my head. *Shut it*, I tell her.

I perfected Lulu after watching the film *To Sir, with Love* five times, then briefly tried on Diana Rigg from a television show called *The Avengers*. Recently I mastered Twiggy the pop star, my best act yet. Sunny says that as Twiggy, I sparkle and conquer. My sister's right. It moved me to center stage.

The performing started after we returned from Ghana. I noticed that my three other Bengali classmates had grown quieter and even less social than before I left. It was as if they'd been pushed into an audience while I'd been gone. If our school were a theater, the Bengali girls were invisible now, high up in the balcony seats somewhere. I didn't want to join them, admiring British-born actors who loved, cried, fought, and lived while we applauded. Nobody was going to shove a Das girl into the cheap seats. That's when I became Lulu, and then Diana. Twiggy was my last and greatest transformation.

But staying on center stage takes work—lots of work. I have to study, imitate, and rehearse until one magical moment when I move into another person's skin. And Twiggy's not going to work in America.

I switch on the television, rotate the channel dial through the four channels, and settle on a serialized show called *All My Children*. Reaching for the model Big Ben clock that we brought along from London, I set an alarm for ten minutes from now.

"What are we sharing this time?" Sunny asks, still not looking up from her book.

I hand her the magazine. "Fanning duty. Ten minutes you. Ten minutes me."

Sunny flaps and reads, and the breeze she makes begins to cool my cheeks. Meanwhile, I watch *All My Children* intently, remembering the techniques my friend Melissa passed on to me. She was a decent actor, and one of Mrs. Campbell's favorites. Our magnificent theater teacher in London didn't even know I could act. What was the point of trying out for her shows? Ma wants me to have a career, but there are only two possibilities on her list. *Don't make my mistake and give all the money-making power to your husband,* she says. *Study hard and become an engineer. Or a doctor.* Sunny has the grades for both those jobs, so she doesn't have to worry. Unfortunately, I'm no star student. Far from it, in fact. I can imagine the over-the-top reaction if I choose theater as a career. Educated Bengali girls don't act. When we're too dumb for medicine or engineering, they marry us off. Fast.

But what's the use of worrying about that now? I still have two more years of high school, and I'm planning to exit to a standing ovation.

I focus on the television, paying attention to how mouths shape the flatter American sounds and that rolling *r*. I sing along with advertisement jingles. Strange how Brits and Americans sound alike when they sing.

I home in on two characters in the show: Erica, the villain, and Tara, the sweeter one, who shares my name. I always think of myself as "Tara," even though Baba calls me "Star." And I've always been "Starry" to Sunny. Ma calls me "Ma," thanks to a weird Bengali tradition where an older person calls a younger person by the title the younger person is supposed to use for the older person—sort of an affectionate play on words, I guess.

Big Ben chimes. My turn to fan. Television Tara, naïve with a hint of a tough core, is a better possibility than Television Erica. I put her on a mental short list, set the alarm again, and take the magazine.

"Can't you turn the volume down?" Sunny asks. "It's so annoying. Two silly women fighting over a man. Who watches this show, anyway?"

I shrug, get up, and mute the television. The overly dramatic gestures make the plot easy to follow even without a soundtrack. Outside in the playground, I can hear the hydrant dancers we saw earlier. Their flattened accents carry up into our apartment from three stories below.

"Get off that swing! You're too old!"

Another girl laughs. "I'm seventeen! Eric, come push me."

"Hands off my man!" It's the first girl's voice again.

A deep voice calls out. "I can swing with two ladies at once."

Something about their easy give-and-take makes me tired. Why do I have to start all over again? Twiggy was working just fine in London. I stop fanning before Big Ben releases me and turn the volume knob up, louder this time.

She's so caught up in *Little Women*, Sunny doesn't notice that I've stopped fanning or that Television Erica is throwing herself into Television Tara's husband's arms. My sister's in nineteenth-century Massachusetts, where it's cool and safe. I watch to the end of *All My Children*, but by then even Television Tara doesn't seem right. The new incarnation of me has to be perfect. American to the core. Sweet, pretty, but not over-the-top sexy. I can't pull sexy off—not with Baba's strict, loving eyes watching so closely. Besides, after that nighttime visit in London, I'm not interested in attracting a dangerous audience.

The television announces that it's time for *The Brady*

Bunch to air, so I sit back and watch closely. The librarian was right. The Brady family doesn't live in a Flushing flat—*apartment*, I mean—that feels like it's on fire. In her spacious (air-conditioned, probably) house, Mrs. Brady is a lighthearted blonde who bakes chocolate chip cookies; manages her hired hand, Alice; and organizes birthday parties for her children. Mr. Brady is her ideal match—a handsome, kindly architect who offers advice to any of their children in need. And there are three Brady daughters—Marcia, Jan, and Cindy.

I concentrate on Marcia, sweet-but-strong Marcia, flinging her long blond hair around, captivating eyes every time she comes on-screen.

Marcia Brady.

Power oozes from every American pore of her skin.

I sit up with a surge of energy.

"Found the next Starry?" Sunny asks, glancing up at the screen.

"She's perfect," I answer. "Don't you think?"

My sister's eyes follow Marcia for a minute or two. "She'll do."

For the next three weeks, while Baba goes to and from his job, and my sister reads and writes in that diary of hers, I focus on Marcia. I watch her move, talk, laugh, and cry. Ma also joins me to watch *The Brady Bunch* for half an hour before bending over the cloth, shears in hand. I feel hopeful. Our mother's a sewing genius.

I set my hair free from the Twiggy bun, part it in the middle, and let it hang loose. Thank goodness it's long and silky. I glance at my sister, curled up on the couch, sweating and reading, sweating and reading.

"Time to do your hair," I tell her. "Sit up."

She groans. "Can I keep reading?"

"You bet," I say. I sound American already.

I dab the sweat off Sunny's forehead, take the comb, and part her hair in the middle, too. My sister keeps reading. I try to braid it, but her curls keep slipping out of my fingers. She turns another page and shifts around a bit.

"Sit still," I say. "I'm trying to Cindy-Brady you. We're almost there."

She throws me a look over her shoulder, and I smile. We both know that all Cindy Brady and my sister have in common is curly hair, and there's nothing I can do to change that. Sunny is always Sunny—alone, at school, at home when she's with Ma, Baba, and me. With her first-class brain, her writing, and all those books, nobody can make my sister take a seat in the balcony. I picture her in a front-row seat, scribbling reviews that make or break the shows, vanishing at intermission while the actors' hearts break.

"I'm glad we're in the same school," I say, and drop a kiss on her head. In London we were enrolled in different schools because Sunny's so gifted. Here there's no separate school for extra-smart students, and she's coming in as a freshman, as they say, while I'll be a junior. With her around, I'll be sure to have one set of admiring eyes at least.

Two weeks till school starts, and then one. I watch the show daily and practice my Marcia, but my usual tricks aren't working.

Maybe the right costume will help.

I look over the outfits Ma has managed to finish. I like the lime-green pants that end in a flare, the blue and lime-green blouse, the pencil-slim orange dress with the big collar. But none of them seem right for the first day. At the last minute, I convince Ma to make me a powder-blue blouse and a navy miniskirt with a fringe that swirls around Marcia's white thighs. Thankfully, Baba provided reams of dark- and light-blue material. Two days before school starts, Ma hands me a replica of Marcia's eye-catching outfit. She's whipped up a matching skirt-and-blouse set in Sunny's size as well. Amazing.

Sunny holds up the skirt first, and then the shirt, shaking her head. I know what my sister is thinking. "The skirt's too short and the shirt's too tight," she says. "I can tell without trying them on."

Ma is stern. "You'll both wear this on your first day. I measured you, remember?"

"I will never—" My sister catches my pleading look and stops with a sigh. "Oh, all right then. I didn't expect to miss that stupid skirt I had to wear in London but at least it was longer than this. My bottom might make an appearance when I drop something."

I give her a kiss, put on my outfit, and pose in front of the mirror in Ma's room. It's not just leg that draws the eye—the nylon fabric of the blouse clings to my small breasts. Sunny is definitely going to hate this blouse. She'll wear it untucked, I'm sure.

"I can't go to the movies, Jeff," I tell the girl in the mirror. "I have to work at Haskell's Ice Cream Hut."

The costume is right and the accent is decent, but something still feels off. The magic hasn't arrived yet. I feel another pang of worry. School starts the day after tomorrow. What else can I do to get ready? I frown at the scuffed Oxfords on my feet. Maybe *all* the props have to be perfect.

That afternoon, while watching the show, I point out the platform shoes on Marcia's feet to Ma. "Ask your Baba," she says, as predicted.

So I bring the subject up at dinner. I hate to do this to Baba but I'm desperate. "Do you think we can afford new shoes, Baba?"

Ma leaps in with her lines right away. "Your father's paychecks are not that big. We barely have enough for new underwear after he sends money to his mother every month."

Baba sighs, and I fight back my guilt.

"We don't need shoes, Baba," Sunny says, shooting me a hard look. "I've seen both girls and boys wearing Oxfords around here."

"What kind of shoes do you want, my Star?" Baba asks wearily.

"Platform shoes," I say. "They have a three-inch sole all around. They're very stylish."

"I picked up those sequined sandals for you girls in Singapore," Baba says. "They reminded me of the ones my sisters used to wear. What happened to those?"

"We outgrew them, Baba," I say gently. Three years ago.

"Okay, Star. I'll see what I can do."

"I'm fine with Oxfords, Baba," Sunny adds.

"Get some for Baby, too," Ma says. "A girl's clothes must show that she is from an educated family—a good family."

"I said I'd try," Baba says curtly.

"That's what you always say. Doesn't he, girls?"

Sunny leaves the table. I try to change the subject. "How's work going, Baba?"

"I might be getting a raise soon," he tells me, face brightening.

"So you can send more money to Calcutta?" Ma asks. "I thought we were saving for a house."

"We are. But you know my mother is sick, Ranee."

"What about your daughters? We have to get them out of this neighborhood, I tell you . . ."

I manage to swallow one more bite of rice and lentils. Then I leave the kitchen to rehearse my Marcia.

It's here. Opening day.

Ma hands us the powder-blue blouses and navy miniskirts, which she ironed the night before.

Once again, Sunny looks at the clothes with distaste. "Do we have to match? It all seems a bit much, doesn't it?"

"I need you to look like sisters today," Ma says.

Sunny releases one of her signature groans but gets dressed. Sure enough, she leaves her blouse untucked. I head to the mirror and try tying mine at the waist. No, that isn't right. I tuck it in again, but there's still no Marcia in sight. Finally, like my sister, I leave it hanging loose, but my reflection still shows Tara Das, and Tara Das only. This can't be happening. I won't survive this day without the magic. *Come on, Marcia*, I urge. But there's no response. The flat-chested, big-lipped foreigner in the mirror looks scared.

Our Oxfords are waiting by the door. They're going to look terrible with this outfit. As I'm about to slip them on, Baba comes out of the bedroom, holding something in his hands. Platform sandals! Two pairs! Hope rises again.

"I picked them up in a secondhand shop on my way home yesterday," he says, handing me my shoes first. "A first-day present for my girls."

"I gave him your sizes," Ma adds. "They're not new, but they look decent."

"They're perfect, Baba! Thank you so much."

He smiles and hands Sunny her pair. My sister looks them over. I know they look high and wobbly to her, but she slips her feet into them because they're a gift from Baba.

He reaches for Sunny's hand to steady her and clasps it inside both of his. "You'll do just fine today, Mishti. Let your sweetness shine."

She grins at him, and it *is* sweet.

Then he tips up my chin. "May your first day be a success, my Star."

If I can become Marcia in half an hour. "I'll try, Baba."

"It will be," Ma answers, handing him the tiffin box of lunch she packs in the mornings. "That's *my* job."

She's still wearing her nightgown, and Baba's eyes linger on her face and body. To my amazement, Ma holds her pose and lets him look. For a long minute. And then: "I'll wear that lovely green sari you bought in New Delhi."

"You'll outshine your daughters, Ranee," Baba says, eyes following Ma as she heads to the bedroom. When she's no longer in sight, he checks his watch and claps his forehead. "I'll miss my train!" Blowing us kisses, he dashes out the door.

Sunny and I practice in the platform shoes while Ma gets ready. For me, they're fairly easy to manage from the start. They make me feel even more slender and tall. Sunny, though, is taking small steps and teetering along, clutching the sofa for support. I imitate her with big gestures, hugging the back of the armchair while I squat on the floor, shaking and trembling, and toppling over with my platform sandals straight up in the air. Sunny giggles, and I feel the snarl of anxiety loosen a bit.

"You going to be okay?" my sister asks. "You look great on the outside."

"That's not what matters." We both know I have to be Marcia from the inside out, not just look like her.

Meanwhile, Ma has been wrapping and tucking the green silk sari around her slim waist. She's applied lipstick and eye pencil, twisted a dozen golden bangles on each wrist, strung two necklaces around her throat, and selected a pair of dangly earrings. Even though she looks beautiful, I can't help thinking of the simple dress that Mrs. Brady wore during yesterday's show. I say nothing, but Sunny doesn't hold back.

"Do you have to get so dressed up, Ma?" she asks.

"A woman must look her best for the important events in life," Ma answers. "You will learn that today."

She dabs away imaginary crumbs from Sunny's grimace and then turns to appraise me. "You look fine," she tells me, smiling. "It seems like yesterday that I was seventeen. I was already considering suitors by then."

The knot in my stomach tightens again.

"We're going to be late," Sunny calls from the door.

I'm not ready! I need more time! But we have to leave.

The playground is empty. The sidewalks are packed with students striding, skipping, slouching toward school. I stay close to Ma, praying for magic before we reach our destination.

Sunny, I can tell, is enjoying being Sunny. She's liking the feel of the September morning breeze against her cheeks. Leaning into it, she leads the way along the five straight, short blocks, picking up the pace as she masters the sandals. Her blouse billows behind her like a sail and curls escape her braid to dance on her shoulders. I fight a twinge of envy.

We're here. The curtain opens.

Trios and pairs of students greet each other before disappearing inside a crowded lobby. Platform shoes. Miniskirts. Bell-bottomed, high-waisted pants. Tie-dyed T-shirts. The halls are filled with color. The faces around us are mostly brown, with a few white ones sprinkled here and there like salt. Afros abound, music's playing through the intercom, and a river of students swirls around us.

Enter, stage left. We push our way through the crowd. Staying close to Ma's sari, I take Sunny's hand. I can't help hearing the whispers and snickers that come our way. *Why are they laughing? Is it because we're Indian? Because we look so different? Or is it Ma's sari and the dot on her forehead?* Ma *is* drawing attention, but people are also staring at us, at Sunny and me. I see us through their eyes. Our matching skirts and blouses and shoes are stylish, but because they're identical, they highlight how different the two of us look. And nobody in the school is holding hands, at least not two girls who look absolutely nothing like sisters. I should have remembered what we learned on our way to the library that first day in America: teenaged girls don't hold hands. I ease my fingers out of Sunny's and she doesn't hold on.

The receptionist's greeting is as crisp as her red blouse and black skirt. A pair of reading glasses dangle around her neck. She's white, like the librarian. "Good morning." Her eyes take in Ma's silk sari and golden jewelry. "Do you understand our language?"

"Of course we do," answers Ma, speaking slowly in her heavily accented English. "We are coming here from India. It was a British colony, just like America. Most recently we have been living in England." In London, most people were used to Indian accents, even if they didn't like them much. Here, Ma's English sounds odd, with tones that swing up and down and *t*'s formed with a tongue-flick on the roof of the mouth.

"Oh. Okay, then." The receptionist forces a smile. "We don't have too many people from India at the high school yet, but I understand our elementary school recently enrolled several families."

"Your government has issued a change in visa regulations a few years back," Ma informs her. "So I presume more and more of us will be arriving, and then your school will have to educate us."

The receptionist's smile disappears. "Is that so? Well, on to more pressing matters—your daughters' placements. My, they don't even look like sisters, do they? If it wasn't for those matching outfits . . ." She glances from me to Sunny, then back to Ma. "Mr. Daniels has asked to test your oldest daughter first."

Ma narrows her eyes. "My youngest will be tested first. The oldest will wait here."

There's a short silence as the receptionist decides whether or not to challenge this. Then she shrugs. "Follow me, please." Her heels click across the tile floor.

Ma rustles after her. Sunny follows, sending me an encouraging look over her shoulder, and the door swings closed behind them.

I need some Marcia Magic, and I need it now. I move to a bench in the corner of the office, take a deep breath, and get to work. *It's all in the head, Star,* I tell myself.

That's where the magic happens.

Sonia

The Queen of Bargaining

THE RECEPTIONIST USHERS MA AND ME INTO the principal's office, and I stop short at the sight of the man behind the desk. *Oh my goodness.* He's a godsend. The person who rules this school looks *exactly* like Mr. Brady. He's tall and handsome, white and relaxed, with the same dark, curly hair and shining teeth. Exactly what Starry needs.

"Principal Daniels, here's the Das family," the receptionist announces. "This is Ranee Das and her younger daughter, Sonia."

He welcomes us with Mr. Brady's confident smile, speaking slowly, enunciating each word clearly. "Welcome to our community, Mrs. Das. Please sit down. Sonia, my dear, welcome. Do you have a nickname?"

I'm still amazed by this unexpected gift for Starry. Ma nudges me and mutters a command to speak. *"Bol!"*

I gather my wits. "I prefer to be called 'Sonia.' It's quite an easy name for everyone—Indians, Brits, and Americans, too, I hope."

He hides his surprise at my British, no-trace-of-India accent and quickens the pace of his words. "A name that crosses borders easily, eh? Much like the bearer, I think. We're glad you're here, Sonia. Shall we begin the testing?"

We start with math and science. "Perfect," the principal says after checking my answers. "Reading next."

Ma smiles complacently as the principal hands me a book.

"Read aloud, please," he says.

The book is *Betsy-Tacy*, written by a woman named Maud Hart Lovelace. I've never read it, but the words are easy. *Does he think I can't read?* I shrug off my irritation and keep turning pages. It's a tale told well, like all good stories, and it doesn't take long to lose myself in early twentieth-century Minnesota.

After only one chapter, the principal lifts a hand. "Stop!" he orders.

I obey, almost dropping the book. Why is his voice so sharp? Have I said or done something wrong? Ma stirs in her chair, frowning.

But Mr. Brady II is pulling down another book from his shelf and handing it to me. It's called *To Kill a Mockingbird*. "Read this one."

I open the book. "When he was nearly thirteen, my brother Jem got his arm badly broken at the elbow. When it healed, and Jem's fears of never being able to play football were assuaged, he was seldom self-conscious . . ."

"Hold it!" exclaims the principal again, interrupting me.

He's really agitated now, and I still have no idea why. Mr. Brady never gets this worked up on the show. The principal pulls another book off his shelf and almost shoves it into my hands. This one I just finished for the tenth or so time—*Little Women*. I open to the first chapter, but I don't even need to look at the page. I know the first lines by heart. "'Christmas won't be Christmas without any presents,' grumbled Jo, lying on the rug," I recite from memory. Oh, how I love fierce, feisty, feminist Jo!

"Wait just a minute, please," says Mr. Daniels, and presses the intercom. "Get in here. And bring the others."

"What are you doing?" Ma whispers, glaring at me. "Read properly!"

"I was!" I skim the words I've just read. *"Christmas won't be Christmas without any presents," grumbled Jo, lying on the rug.* Am I doing something wrong? Something un-American?

Mr. Daniels smiles reassuringly. "It's okay, Sonia," he says. "Keep reading. Let's hear just a page or two more."

Maybe I haven't made a cultural blunder. I start reading again. It takes a few lines but soon I'm sitting with the March sisters in their drawing room on a wintry afternoon. When I look up after two pages, I'm surprised by a row of grown-ups gazing at me. Something about them reminds me of the pigeons that perch on the railing of the fire escape outside our apartment.

The receptionist is half-seated on the edge of the principal's desk, one hand cupping a cheek, elbow propped up by the other hand. "Keep going, dear," she says. Her voice has lost its sharp edges.

I can't forget myself in a story with so many Americans hearing my every breath. I manage to get through another paragraph and then look up, half-expecting my audience to fly off with a rustle of wings. But none of them move. They're in some kind of trance.

"That lovely British accent!" the receptionist murmurs, breaking the silence.

Another woman takes a handkerchief from her pocket

and dabs at her eyes. "One of my favorite novels when I was a girl," she explains apologetically. "And you read it so beautifully, with such *cadence* and *meaning*."

The principal ushers the spectators out. Before the door swings shut again, I try to catch a glimpse of my waiting sister. Maybe she'll see Mr. Brady II! But the door closes too quickly.

Mr. Daniels turns to Ma with a wide smile. "Sonia will be a wonderful addition to our ninth grade. Unfortunately, we don't have room in our gifted track or we'd put her there."

Ma rises. She takes her time to answer. "Ranee" means queen, and right now she's reminding me of one. "If my daughters are qualifying for a special program of some sort, they should be placed in those classes only." She lets the English words roll out slowly, emphasizing each phrase with a figure-eight head movement. "Their father and I desire them to face the highest of challenges. And Sonia wants to continue with advanced French. She's excellent with languages."

The principal flashes his best Brady grin. "I'm sure a brilliant girl like Sonia will shine no matter where she's placed. I might be able to squeeze her into Advanced French, but the gifted classes are full this semester, Mrs. Das. At *all* the grade levels. I'm sorry. There's no room for either of your girls."

Another long pause. And then: "*Both* of my daughters are talented, sir. And *both* must be placed in these gifted classes."

The principal stops smiling. He sits, pulls open a file drawer, takes out a folder and flips through the contents. Ma doesn't move. The folds of her sari are as still as stone. I watch in awe. *If she lifts one arm*, I think, *she'll look exactly like the statue in the harbor.*

"We might be able to squeeze Sonia into the ninth-grade gifted class," Mr. Daniels says finally. "But there's definitely no room in the eleventh-grade gifted class for your other daughter. Those students have been together for two years now, and the class is already too large."

Ma's face breaks into a smile, and her sari rustles as she taps her palms together in a Namaste. It sounds like one short clap of applause to me. "Thank you, Mr. Daniels," she says sweetly.

The principal seems confused, and I feel a pang of pity. He's never watched our mother barter over fish and spices in Indian grocery stores. How is he supposed to know that Ma always gets her price?

He turns to me. "Sonia, will you bring your sister in for her evaluation? I'll have to ask you to wait outside while I test her."

"Certainly. May I borrow these?" I pick up *Betsy-Tacy* and *To Kill a Mockingbird*.

"Of course, but take good care of them. That copy of Lovelace's book was my mother's. She read the whole series aloud to us when we were children. Let me know what you think."

We shake hands with him and walk out to the reception area. My sister rises from a bench in the corner, and I can tell immediately that something is different. Just by the way she stands, by the confident smile she flashes as she walks to meet us, I can tell she's almost there. Wait until she sees who's inside. I take her by the hand, lead her to the door, hold it open, and step aside to give her a good view of the principal.

She stops for a second at the sight of him, and then it happens. Marcia Das flips her hair over her shoulders and enters the principal's office. For a second, as the light shimmers on the shiny black cascade of my sister's hair, I'm almost sure I see a glint of blond.

Sonia

Fire Escape

WE'VE BEEN IN THE LAND OF THE FREE for four months and Ma continues to forbid me from going out alone. Baba doesn't over-rule her. In my captivity, I haven't been able to write much. Ma lets Starry and me go to the library once a week, but only for an hour. I write some there, but even with only my sister nearby the words don't come as easily. Unless I'm alone—without another member of the Das family around—my thoughts don't spill across the page. And when they get stuck inside me, they simmer and boil. I worry they might even explode.

Thank goodness I've found a private writing place inside

the apartment. Technically, it's outside the apartment, but I don't have to walk out the front door to get to it. And yet it still feels hundreds of miles away. *A Tree Grows in Brooklyn* gave me the idea. If a fire escape was a haven for Francie back then, why couldn't it serve the same purpose for me in 1973?

Outside our bedroom window, my sanctuary waits—airy and open, made of red railings and blue sky. At first I stole a few moments out here, savoring them like forbidden delicacies. But as the weeks pass, my need to write keeps growing.

I climb out on the fire escape almost every afternoon now, writing while the sparrows dance against the darkening sky. One ladder leads down to the next floor, and another heads up and up, as high as the roof. Thanks to a tall tree, nobody can see me from the playground below. And the curtains, which I pull closed behind me, block the view from inside our bedroom.

My only complaint has been that the railings are too hard to sit on for very long. But yesterday I found a faded quilt in a pile of giveaways in our apartment building's laundry room. I sink into the softness of it and peek down through the railing. Thank goodness—no sign of Gerald doing a terrible Romeo imitation on the sidewalk below. It takes a while for me to make friends—Samantha and Elsa and I were in class three together and we didn't become close until class seven.

My only American friend so far is an eighth-grade boy with a voice that's higher than mine, and he still keeps trying to move us into romantic territory. Gerald's sweet and even funny sometimes, but he's no Mr. Darcy, that's for sure.

Meanwhile, it's no surprise that guys are falling hard for Marcia Das. Starry's inside our room; I can hear her singing "Got to Be There" as she pretends to study. Karen and Jenny, two of her new friends in the neighborhood, are also music lovers. While we walk home from school, the three of them sing hits by groups like the Jackson 5, Al Green, and the Stylistics. I open my diary.

The fights have started again. Anger fills the corners of our apartment like a bad smell. Ma starts nagging right when Baba gets home from work—

"Hey, Women's Rights! You up there? Want to go to White Castle?"

I sigh. I don't want to interrupt my writing to chat. Or to reject him again. This child actually thinks he has a chance. I might be flattered if I weren't so annoyed. I lean back against the brick wall. Out of sight, out of mind. I can't answer anyway. If Ma heard me, she'd never let me come out here again.

"I'll pay for a milkshake. You can borrow my sister's bike."

I stay quiet. *Go away, little man.*

One more try from below: "I'll even buy us cheeseburgers!"

I don't risk moving until I'm certain he's gone. Then I take the cap off my pen and start writing. Words are springing up inside me; I've been waiting all day to spill them across the page.

Last night Baba talked again about moving to Calcutta after Starry's graduation. My sister's marks—I mean grades—aren't improving. For once, Ma, Starry, and I joined forces. Moving back to India would be our doom—the two of us married off to "suitable" Bengali boys and Ma stuck in a small flat with a mother-in-law she hates. No escape.

Talk about being stuck in a flat. Ma won't let me stay after school, even though several girls have invited me to join the Equal Rights Club. I thought life in America might be different. But no. I'm in captivity

My sister's voice calls from inside the apartment. "Sunny! Ma wants you! Come help with the laundry!"

Sighing, I mark my place mid-sentence with a semicolon, tuck the pen and notebook under the quilt, and climb back into our bedroom. Starry is waiting, arms crossed, a worried pucker on her forehead. "You really shouldn't climb out there, Sunny. It's too dangerous."

"It's not. It's wonderful."

"She'll find out sooner or later. She always does."

"Not if I can help it."

Starry shrugs. "I'll cover for you. But please be careful."

It's breezy on the roof, where the three Bengali families in our building hang their clothes to dry. Ma is removing clothespins from the half-emptied line. "Where were you?" she asks me.

"Starry found me," I answer, reaching quickly for a dry towel to fold.

Ma shakes her head but doesn't say anything. We focus on our task. The autumn afternoon is fading quickly. My sister and I battle the breeze to fold sheets, stepping together to make the corners meet, backing up less and less each time to form the shrinking rectangle.

The door to the roof opens and a neighbor emerges, the oldest of the three Bengali wives in the building. I nudge my sister and we duck behind a sari floating on the line.

It was through this "auntie"—a woman with loose connections to our family back in Calcutta—that Baba found the apartment. Her one asset is music, so our father hired her as

Starry's music teacher. With no children around and not much to do, this neighbor spends her time exploring other people's business. Mainly ours. She likes to pull us aside and ask sweetly why our parents are fighting again. I've labeled her "Big Harm" behind her back—short for the harmonium she plays—and her husband is "Little Harm," because he's shorter, skinnier, and slightly less evil than his wife. Even my sister's taken to calling them "Auntie Harm" and "Uncle Harm" in private. Starry manages to stick to "Auntie" when she addresses this terrible woman, but she's always worried that the Harm's going to slip out. It hasn't yet.

Ma scolded us when she overheard the nickname. She told us that this sour woman's one daughter disappeared years ago, and never calls or writes. The rumor is that Harm Junior moved to California and became a hippie. *More power to her*, I say. I might just follow in her footsteps. But I don't tell Ma that.

Flinging our cotton barrier aside, Big Harm corners us. Grabbing Starry's chin, she swivels my sister's head from side to side, as though looking for bruises on a mango. "What a beauty," she says in Bangla. "You'll have no trouble finding a husband. Take care of that lovely skin, keep it out of the sun."

"I will, Auntie," Starry answers, perfectly and politely. But in English.

Then the woman turns to me. Instinctively, I step out of reach of her hard fingers. Tara looked down during the scrutiny, but I meet Big Harm's gaze with narrowed eyes. I don't blame her daughter one bit for escaping this tyranny.

Ma comes to stand beside me, and our intruder makes a clucking sound of disapproval. "This one worries me, Ranee. She's very secretive."

Am I invisible? An object instead of a person? Why talk about *me instead of* to *me?* It takes every shred of self-control not to confront this woman. But I can't shame Ma.

The woman's eyes roam down my body and return to my face. "And her skin is so black! Americans probably don't even recognize her as a Bengali."

This time I can't stop myself. "You mean they might think I'm black? That's wonderful! I'll fit right in." I roll up my sleeves and stretch my dark, strong forearms into the space between us, right under Harm's nose.

Ma's sharp, quick elbow hits my side like a bullet. "Your sister needs help, Baby."

It's the term of endearment that makes me obey, not the elbow. I stalk past the woman and head over to Starry, who's struggling against the wind to fold another sari.

We can still hear Big Harm's sharp voice. "You see? She's already becoming less like a Bengali girl. Speaking all the time in English. And so rudely, at that. The students in that school are a bad influence. How will you raise a girl like that in such a place?"

"We're not staying here for long," Ma answers quickly. "We're moving to New Jersey very soon." But she doesn't defend me.

"That's what I thought," says the woman. "It's been four years for us and we still haven't moved. They don't give promotions to Indians. Your husband is just like mine—all talk and no money in the bank."

I choke back my words, waiting for Ma to answer. *Defend Baba! Stand up for him!* But she stays quiet. With an impatient yank, she tugs another sari off the line.

Starry sees my face. "Go downstairs," she tells me. "Right now."

I barrel to the exit, praying Ma won't stop me.

"Off to study again, Baby?" she calls.

I nod, my hand on the knob. Almost there. I pull the door open.

"She gets top marks in all of her classes," Ma is saying. If only her tone weren't so apologetic. "She's in the gifted program, you know—"

The door closes behind me, silencing their voices. I head down to our apartment and walk past the kitchen, where the table is set for dinner. Steam rises from the rice cooker, and semicircles of eggplant are sliced and ready to sizzle in the frying pan. Baba's working overtime again. He'll be tired, his defenses down. Probably another fight night.

I climb back out to my hiding place. On the fire escape, a cold, quiet breeze greets me. There's just enough light left to write; the anger won't subside until I release my words. Better here, in my diary, where they can't destroy anyone.

She's to blame for our family falling apart. Why can't she see how hard Baba is trying? He asks me to give her respect and honor, but how can you respect and honor someone who doesn't return it? She values my success in school, but only because it elevates her social status. What if I did run away? I don't think I can stand this prison of an apartment much longer. But think of Baba and Starry; I could never do that to them. No, I'm stuck here. The worst part of it, the very worst, is that deep inside I still love her. I may not like her much, but I can't help loving her.

Inside the kitchen, somebody switches on a light. "Did your sister have to be so rude?"

"You know how she feels about that auntie," Starry answers.

"Terrible woman! Giving her opinion on everything. But your sister *is* secretive. I don't understand it. Pass the salt, will you?"

A door slams and Baba's voice joins the conversation. "Something smells wonderful. Where's Mishti?"

"Hi, Baba," Starry answers. "I think she's in our room."

My sister's soft voice summons me again. "Time for dinner, Sunny!"

Baba's already eating when we join him. Ma hovers around us, heaping rice and yellow lentils on our plates. In the village where she grew up, the women ate together after the men and the children were done. They still do that in my grandmother's house—gathering in the kitchen, chatting and laughing, celebrating the end of another day's work. Here, Ma eats alone. She waits until we're asleep and Baba heads to bed.

They're not fighting yet, but she's muttering as she dips the eggplant slices in batter and begins frying them. "Sending half his paycheck to his mother. What does that leave for us?"

Enough, I think. *We never go hungry. We always have shelter. Starry is the best-dressed girl in school.*

Baba stays quiet, but my temperature's rising.

The spatula slaps an eggplant slice onto Baba's plate. "My cousin Ruma's husband is the top engineer in his firm. They live in that big house outside London. Now *there's* a man who provides—"

"Enough!" I stand and bang both palms on the table. "Baba provides just fine! So many of his friends in London still can't find permanent jobs—he found one as soon as he got here."

"Mishti!" Baba's anger is hardly ever directed at me, and I flinch at his tone.

Starry pats my chair. "Sit down, Sunny," she hisses, and after one look at Baba's face, I do.

"This kind of behavior is exactly what I'm talking about," Ma says. "Our girls are getting ruined."

"There's talk at work about giving me a promotion," Baba says. "Soon we'll be able to leave Flushing and buy a house. In New Jersey, the schools are better—"

"We'd be able to move there NOW if you hadn't given away so much of our money—"

Don't say anything, don't say anything, I chant in my head. But now it's Baba who can't hold back his words: "Money! That's all you talk about. What kind of example are you to our daughters?"

Ma puts one hand to her throat, and I can see her fingers tremble. She puts a hand on Starry's shoulder. "Did you hear that? Tell him to stop talking like this, Ma. Tell him how much it upsets you. Go on, tell him."

Starry looks at our father glowering at the head of the table. "Baba—" she manages to whisper, before stopping.

I leap to my feet. "Leave Starry out of it! This is your fight, not ours."

Before our parents can react, I grab my sister's hand and pull her into our bedroom. We collapse on our beds.

"Sunny, you shouldn't have yelled at Ma. It just makes it harder for Baba."

"I know, I know." The voices in the kitchen are louder and angrier than ever. *Another beautiful day in America for the Das family*, I think.

Starry reaches over to the nightstand between us and turns on the radio. "Oooh, good song. Come on, Sunny, sing with me." But I don't want to. I'm still seething with anger and sadness from dinner. My heart feels sore. She flops back on the bed and starts singing: "War, good God now, what is it good for?"

I glance over at my sister as she sings. Her face is tired, but her eyes are wide, reflecting the small lamp between our beds.

"Absolutely nothing! Say it again." Her voice makes even a loud rock 'n' roll song sound sweet.

Still singing, my sister reaches across the small space between our beds.

I take her hand. What else can I do? Staring up at the popcorn ceiling over our heads, I join in. It *is* a good song. "War, what is it good for? Absolutely nothing, listen to me . . ." I'm off-key, but together our voices drown out the fighting.

The next day, it starts to rain as we head home from school. Starry leaves her friends behind and jogs to keep up with me. "What's your hurry today?"

"I left my notebook on the fire escape. It's going to get soaked."

"It's not raining that hard yet," Starry says, but she quickens her steps.

"Can you distract her while I bring it in?" I ask. Ma usually has cups of steaming tea and biscuits waiting. Then she sits at the kitchen table with us until we finish our homework.

"I'll try."

When we get home, Starry heads straight for the kitchen. But today Ma isn't there. She's standing by the open window in our bedroom with my wet notebook in her hand. My quilt, soaked by rain, lies in a heavy heap at her feet. Tears streak her cheeks, but as soon as she sees me, she wipes them away.

My heart plummets. My words! How many has she read?

"What are you doing?" I demand. "Give that to me."

Starry is right behind me. "Ma! That's Sunny's!"

"I was closing the window so the rain wouldn't come in," Ma says, still holding the notebook. "I saw some things out there."

"Did you read it?" My voice is shaking. Did she read the last bit I wrote—about not liking her? It's true, but those words weren't meant for her eyes. Or her heart.

She doesn't meet my eye. "Have you been sitting out there, Baby? It's not safe."

"I said, *did you read it?*"

She hands me my notebook, and stoops to gather up the quilt. "Where did you find this rag?"

I squeeze my words tightly in my hand. "In the laundry room. How much did you read?"

"And you brought it in here? A dirty, used thing like this?" Ma's eyes and lips squeeze into a mass of wrinkles around her nose. She shakes her head in disgust.

It's an expression that never fails to defeat me. Now both the notebook and my quilt seem foul, dingy, and ruined, damaged beyond repair. Throwing myself across my bed, I bury my face in my pillow. Starry sits beside me, her hand on my curls. The notebook slips out of my fingers and lands on the carpet.

I hear our mother stride out of the room. Starry gets up and pounds after her. My sister and Ma hardly ever fight, but those footsteps sound like a battle's about to begin. After a minute, I stand up and follow them into the kitchen.

Rain is lashing against the small window. Peering into the dimness, I see Ma and Starry locked in a strange tug-of-war by a small square in the wall. It's the incinerator door, still closed, but leading to a dark, scary room down in the building's basement. I don't like to pass it when I visit the laundry. There's no telling when the creature in there will come to life, snarling and roaring, devouring the trash that comes hurtling down chutes from the apartments above. Yanking the door open, Ma begins to stuff the quilt inside the chute. Meanwhile, Starry is grasping a chunk of the wet, heavy material and struggling to pull it back out. Their faces are illuminated by the fire four stories below us.

I stand numbly as my mother and sister battle over my quilt in a fierce, silent echo of the sheet folding they'd done the day before. Suddenly, with a burst of strength and a wail that surely reaches down to the basement, Ma gives a fierce tug and then a hefty shove. Starry gropes after the material that's been yanked from her hands, but it falls out of reach and the whole quilt tumbles down the chute. I listen as the fire below roars in delight.

My sister and mother are both breathing heavily. Starry recovers first. "You read her diary! That's wrong, Ma!"

Ma closes the incinerator door and raises her palms in the air like she's praying. "I have to find out what's going on in her head, don't I? It's my duty to keep her safe."

"You'll make her dangerous instead," Starry answers.

She strides out of the kitchen without looking back. Even then, Ma doesn't meet my eyes. For a moment, she searches the room, like a lost child in a crowd of strangers. Then she sits down, gathers the flowing end of her sari, drapes it over her head, and hides her face in her arms.

I go back into the bedroom and pick up my wet, half-full notebook. The words have been captured. But they did their job, they helped me survive; I can let them go. Baba's arrival gift waits for me, full of blank, dry pages.

Returning to the kitchen, where Ma is still hiding, I pull the incinerator door open and toss my notebook inside. It tumbles and bangs down the sides of the chute, as if my words are shouting their truth one last time.

Tara

Flushing Forever

GERALD, MY SISTER'S SHADOW, IS SITTING AT our kitchen table helping Sunny make RATIFY! posters for her Equal Rights Club. ERC, they call it, and their main goal is to get the Equal Rights Amendment ratified and added to the Constitution.

"They'll be home any minute," I tell Sunny, tossing the empty milk carton down the incinerator chute. "Get him out of here."

"Skedaddle," she tells him.

"Okay, Babe," Gerald says, blowing her a kiss and heading out.

"DON'T CALL ME 'BABE'!" Sunny yells after him, but

he's already gone. I hope Auntie Harm didn't hear her. Gerald's a smart kid; he tiptoes down the hall. It's Sunny who's going to get us in trouble.

Gerald's crazy enough to come into our apartment, but only when he knows Baba and Ma are out. And anyway, he and Sunny are just friends. Most boys around here—especially the ones who want to be more than friends—are terrified of Baba. Take David, for example. I certainly wouldn't mind if *he* came up when our parents weren't around. But no. "Your dad's a big guy, Tara," David said the other day when I tried to join him on the swing. He pushed me away gently and looked up at our window.

Sunny starts clearing the table. "Eight more states by 1979," she reminds me before heading to our room to put her posters away.

"I know, I know," I mutter, measuring tea into the saucepan.

Since Ma started letting her stay after school, Sunny's ERC friends are getting her even more fired up about women's rights. She makes me tune in to the news every afternoon to watch the feminist protests.

The ERC is not the only thing that changed after Diary Destruction Day. *D-Day*, as Sunny and I call it. To our surprise, Ma stopped nagging Baba almost immediately.

Maybe that's why Baba got less tired-looking and more cheerful. Then, two months ago, he pushed for that promotion and got it. More money in the bank. Enough income for us to apply for a loan.

For the past six Saturday mornings, Baba's borrowed a car, Ma has dressed in a nice sari, and they've driven to New Jersey to find us a house. They usually don't return until late in the afternoon, which gives Sunny and me seven magnificent hours of freedom. We just have to make sure to be back in the apartment well before our parents return. We can't have World War III breaking out. If they were to drive past the park and see me sitting on Eric's lap or sharing a cigarette with Karen, I'd be dead. It's not like I'm going any further with Eric—and the cigarette's just for show. Even Marcia Brady tried it once.

Which reminds me—I'm getting bored of Marcia. She helped me shake off my British accent and survive the first few months here, but I'm thinking of replacing her. Maybe with Thelma from a new show called *Good Times*. Marcia is too bland for this neighborhood, especially on Saturday mornings when we go to Jenny's apartment and a bunch of us dance along to *Soul Train*. Even Sunny dances sometimes. And Gerald's always grooving right next to her, watching her every move.

Oh, how I love Motown. Black music adds soul and rhythm to my world. Baba still makes me take Rabindra Sangeet lessons from Auntie Harm—that hasn't changed. But he and Ma got me a record player for my eighteenth birthday in March plus a couple of albums. A compilation of hits by the Carpenters and a new one from Barbra Streisand called *The Way We Were*. The record-store owner suggested them. I'd have chosen other artists, but I was grateful for the gift. I borrow albums from Karen or Jenny to play—the Stylistics, Al Green, and Marvin Gaye. In return, I transcribe lyrics when I should be studying and slip them into the album covers so we can sing the songs together.

Despite my terrible grades and our parents' strict rules, junior year in Flushing has turned out pretty nicely. There's only one thing missing, but it's a big deal for me: our school has no drama program. If we had one, I could befriend an actor or two, and get them to keep training me on the sly.

Sunny comes back into the kitchen and fans biscuits on a plate. "Think they found something today?"

"Probably not." Our parents have been returning discouraged; all the houses Ma likes are too expensive for Baba, and all the ones he likes are too small or not in "good" neighborhoods.

The door opens.

"How was it?" I ask, pouring them cups of tea.

Ma shakes her head, but Baba has a bounce to his step.

"There *is* one house that would be perfect," he says. "It's in Ridgeford. Near a top high school for you girls."

This is new. A top high school? *With a theater program, maybe?* But Ma is tightening her face into a "no" look. Before she has a chance to speak, Baba hands me a leaflet.

"Let the girls have a peek," he says.

Ma shrugs and reaches for a biscuit while I study the leaflet. White house, single-storied, with a green lawn and a big tree in front of it. Looks okay. Cozy. American. Not quite as big as the Brady house, but there's a slight resemblance.

My sister takes a longer look, reading the details while our parents sip their tea. "Could we plant a garden?" she asks.

"There's a small but sunny patch of land in the back," Baba answers. "We could grow tomatoes and chili peppers, like my mother did in the village."

Sunny tries to hand the leaflet back to Baba, but Ma intercepts it. "It's too small," she says. "Only three bedrooms, two baths. Hardly bigger than this flat."

"It's near a beautiful park." Baba eases the leaflet out of Ma's fingers. "Look, there's a cycling path that goes along the river. I haven't cycled since engineering college."

"But we need something more spacious," Ma says. "We'll keep looking. Let's forget about this one. It's not right."

Baba holds his cup out for more tea, and I fill it. "Star could have one year in that beautiful new high school," he says. "They might help her get into college after graduation. And both girls will be with other students from good families."

Sunny catches my eye; Baba isn't backing down. He's even using Ma's catchphrases.

"College? She doesn't have the marks for college. I still think she should pursue a profession before we arrange her marriage, but I'm starting to lose hope."

"Well, Starry?" Sunny asks, closing her book. "You want Ma and Baba to start arranging your marriage?"

She knows the answer. She's been pestering me to tell our parents the truth, but I don't have her courage. I compromise by starting with the truth and ending with a lie. "No, not just yet. I promise I'll study harder. I want to become an engineer, like you, Baba."

I can't stop the lie that slips from my lips. What else can I do? Like I said, good Bengali daughters have three options after high school: go to college and study engineering, go to college and study medicine, or, if they're pretty but terrible in school like me, *marry* an engineer or a doctor. What if I told them I want to act for a living? Ma would protest that it's a low-class job for uneducated people. Even Baba would probably rather I get married than pursue theater.

Ma snorts. "Engineering? I don't think so. Your marks in maths and science are terrible, Ma. You're eighteen now. My marriage was already fixed by then."

I can see the anger in Sunny bubbling like milk on the stove. That's one thing that D-Day didn't change: fights between Sunny and Ma. If anything, they've intensified. Arguing is still their favorite way to communicate.

"You're not arranging *my* marriage," my sister says. "I'm not even sure I *want* to get married. It's such a patriarchal institution. This is exactly why I'm never going back to India!"

"Indian women could teach your American bra-burners a thing or two," Ma retorts.

Sunny leaps to her feet. "YOU?! What do *you* know about *women's rights*? You just said you were married off at age eighteen!"

"Your *feminists* don't realize that there are different kinds of power," Ma interrupts, her accent taunting the one English word in her sentence.

"And they're all in the hands of men!" Sunny is standing cross-armed in front of Ma, short legs planted widely.

Ma starts a tirade, but Sunny doesn't back down. I tune their argument out and pour myself some tea. Baba and I live with the Bengali female versions of heavyweight boxers Muhammad Ali and Ken Norton. It's a good thing he referees along with me, diverting one or the other, telling a joke, teasing Sunny in just the right way. I look to him now for help as they continue to skirmish, but he's ignoring them. I lean over to see what he's doing; he's scribbling on the leaflet, figuring math problems in the margins.

Baba must sense me watching, because he puts the pencil down. "Listen to me, Ranee," he says, and something in his voice grabs the attention of the fighters. Ma stops talking; Sunny sinks back into a chair. "With the loan and what we've saved for a down payment, we can afford small monthly payments on this house. I even have enough life insurance to cover the mortgage payments if anything were to happen to me—"

"Nothing's going to happen, Baba," Sunny interrupts.

"But in case it does. You'd be able to stay in that house. The girls will have a safe upbringing in that neighborhood. We can always add to it later and make it bigger. What do you think?"

And then he reaches across the table to take Ma's hand

in both of his. He's never done that to Ma—to me and Sunny, yes—but he's never touched our mother in front of us like this.

Ma catches her breath at the shock of it and tries to pull away. But Baba's gripping tightly, encasing her hand with his warm palms. "Please, Ranee. Listen to me this one time. I know this house is right."

She stops trying to free her hand. They gaze into each other's eyes for a long minute. That's unusual, too. Bengali husbands and wives don't look directly at each other in the presence of others. Sunny and I are statues. The only sounds in the kitchen are our Big Ben clock chiming the half hour and the incinerator roaring four floors below.

Finally, Ma breaks the silence. "All right. We will buy this house."

Baba releases her hand, beaming. "You won't regret it, Ranee. This is going to be a beautiful start for our family—owning a home! Our year's lease on this apartment is up in August, so we can get settled just before school begins for the girls. Let me call the real estate agent right now."

The phone's in the living room, so he drops a kiss on my head, and then on Sunny's, and dashes off to buy our first house.

The three of us listen to Big Ben ticking toward five o'clock.

"I'll be glad to stop sending rent checks to that landlord," Ma says finally. "That's one good thing. And we'll get out of Flushing forever."

My sister and I exchange looks. We're just beginning to feel at home here. Sunny loves the library and her new feminist friends, and Karen and Jenny love music almost as much as I do. Our Saturdays of freedom have been fantastic. Eric's fun to flirt with. Even better, sweet David seems to be on the verge of declaring his love for me. For once, I might accept it. *But Ridgeford is only a quick train ride away*, I remind myself. *And if the new school has a theater program—*

"It's high time for us to leave," Ma continues. "I've seen how those Negro boys look at you girls."

Sunny leaps to her feet. "I hate when you talk about our friends like that! It makes you sound like you're from the 1950s! Nobody calls them 'negroes' anymore."

And the two of them are at it again. Round 7,354.

"Negroes, 'black people,' I don't care what they're called," Ma says. "Remember that you girls come from an educated family in Bengal."

"We're not in Bengal anymore. There's no caste system in America. The Declaration of Independence made it clear: 'All men are created equal.' And we'll be changing 'men' to 'people' soon."

"All people are not treated equally," Ma retorts. "It's like that everywhere in the world. In India, people assume that if you have dark skin, you're from a lower caste. Here, it's the same—black people are the lowest caste in this country."

That triggers Sunny to fury. "If it weren't for closed-minded people who keep perpetuating racial stereotypes—!"

Thankfully, Baba comes marching back into the room with both hands high over his head.

"We bought a house!" he announces, beaming at the three of us. "Let's go celebrate! We'll splurge at a restaurant! Fish and chips, my family?"

They're his favorite. "Sounds good, Baba," I say, and step on Sunny's foot under the table.

Sunny takes a deep breath. "Yum," she says, her voice carefully flat. "Can't wait." She's a terrible actress, but Baba doesn't seem to notice.

Ma comes through beautifully, smiling at Baba. "Let me put on a nicer sari," she says. "What a happy day!"

August comes quickly. Time to say goodbye to Flushing. Eric writes a poem about my hair and skin and eyes and lips. It's not bad. And Jenny and Karen promise to visit, and give me the Spinners and the Supremes albums as going-away presents.

But David! David gets all teary-eyed on me.

It's my last Saturday afternoon in Flushing. Ma, Baba, and Sunny have taken a load of things to the new house. David and I are slow-dancing in Jenny's apartment to "Let's Stay Together," and his strong, slim body is pressing hard against mine. I don't pull away.

"I love you, Tara," he whispers near my ear.

I look up and see the tears, and they undo me. He bends his head, I tip mine up, and Al Green's pleading voice becomes the soundtrack to my first sweet, deep kiss.

David's is not the only broken heart we leave behind. Gerald races alongside the rented moving truck as we pull away, waving and shouting, forgetting any Baba-terror in the agony of farewell. "Come back and visit, Sonia! Thanks for the present!"

His voice, sadly, is still a soprano, but he's clutching Sunny's old copy of *Pride and Prejudice*. My sister rolls her eyes but waves back. Ma rolls up her window and doesn't ask questions.

Tara

Star Quality

SOMETHING STRANGE HAPPENS TO OUR PARENTS once we move into the new house. It's like they start dating or something.

On the weekends, after Baba cycles along the river, the two of them tackle the garden side by side, planting mums and seeding new raised beds with beets, radishes, and garlic. Ma sings Rabindra Sangeet for Baba's appreciative ears. Then they take off in a new-to-us 1967 Chevy Nova, hunting for furniture bargains at garage sales and in thrift shops. At night, after dinner, Sunny and I drown out the laughter, soft talking, and long silences coming from behind their closed bedroom door by turning up the television.

Other than the brand-new color television they bought, I don't pay attention to my parents' decorating choices. Their taste is way too Bengali for me. The real estate agent informed us that our new house is a simple Cape Cod. And it still looks like one on the outside, but the inside glitters with mirrored batiks, silk pillows, ornate copper vases full of roses, incense sticks, and altars to Durga, Lakshmi, Kali, and Saraswati, our mother's favorite goddesses. Smells of black pepper, turmeric, ginger, cinnamon, and garlic mingle happily with the scent of new paint. Sunny's thrilled to have a room to herself. "It's not that I don't like sharing with you, Starry, but now I can close the door. It's a feast to be alone in there and write and read without *anyone* coming in."

I don't take it personally. I know she needs alone time. And Ma gives us more freedom here than we had in Flushing. We can walk around Ridgeford anytime we want, alone or together. "There's nothing mysterious about it," Sunny tells me. "It's obvious. The town's full of white people. And a few Indians, like us."

School starts in a week. I wonder if I can muster up the energy to acquire another persona. Maybe I should stay Marcia for one more year. Will she seem as dull as she did in Flushing?

Baba drops the three of us off at the Ridgeford shopping

mall. Ma will still make some of our clothes, and we haven't grown much since last year, but she lets us pick out a few ready-made things. We stick to the clearance racks. Having a bit of extra money hasn't made Ma lose her mind. Sunny grabs her usual jeans and T-shirts, but I find it hard to choose something new. What's going to work at Ridgeford High? What's not? Do I even care anymore? I settle on a plain black skirt and white blouse.

On the first morning of school, Ma begins picking out an appropriate sari for herself. "Does this still suit me?" she asks Baba, holding up one of his favorites—an expensive purple-and-white sari purchased years ago in one of Calcutta's best shops.

"It looks beautiful, but you won't need to wear it," he answers. "I've taken the day off to enroll the girls."

"But that's my duty," Ma says.

"I know you've done it all these years, Ranee, but this is Star's last year and I'd like to take the girls. Is that all right with you two?"

"Definitely, Baba," Sunny answers.

I feel a strange relief. With Baba leading us through the unfamiliar halls, maybe I can stay just Tara Das. At least for the first day.

Oddly, Ma seems glad, too. "Now that Baby has a brilliant record from Flushing, you won't need me there."

What about me? I wonder. My record isn't so stellar.

She hands Sunny and me brown-bag lunches, pats our cheeks gently for luck, and the three of us head out with plenty of time to spare. It feels like a long while since just Sunny, Baba, and I have spent time together.

"Remember when you used to take us to the London Zoo or to Trafalgar Square, Baba?" Sunny asks.

"Some of my favorite memories," Baba says.

We stroll along side by side, our father in the middle. Ridgeford's leafy trees are just starting to turn. Lush green lawns, wide streets, and clean, new sidewalks lead to a small downtown area with a library for Sunny and a record shop for me.

Baba stops in front of a café. "Let's splurge on a few things hot and sweet, shall we, girls? We have time. It's a special day—Star's last first day of high school. A new beginning for both of you."

He makes it feel like a holiday. But that's how it always is with Baba. Clutching cups of coffee and donuts, we round a corner and see the brick school. Ridgeford High is large and new and spacious. Right away, I notice that Sunny and I are among just a few brown and black kids entering the building. The halls inside are packed with Brady girls.

I guess I'll stick with Marcia—might even take her to the next level.

A friendly registrar greets us in the office and looks over Sunny's transcript. "Straight A's in Flushing's gifted program? You'll do just fine here, young lady. I'll enroll you in Advanced Placement for math, English, French, and physics."

I fight a pang of envy. Success is so often measured by grades and test scores. The woman scans my transcript— mostly C's bracketed by a couple of B's and D's. "Are you thinking of college, dear?"

"I hope so."

"We have a terrific community college nearby. We'll just sign you up for the few requirements you'll need to attend there, shall we?"

"Do you offer drama classes at this school?" Sunny asks suddenly.

What is she doing? Baba's right here.

"Oh, yes," the cheerful woman answers. "We have a wonderful theater program and a full-time drama instructor."

My heart jumps. Baba's been standing to the side, letting us handle the enrollment. Now he steps forward. "Are you wanting to take theater, Mishti?" he asks in English, and his voice is surprised.

Sunny lowers her voice so that only he and I can hear. "For Starry."

Baba looks at me and raises his eyebrows. I can't bring myself to answer his unspoken question.

The registrar didn't hear my sister. "There *is* room in the beginning class for freshmen and sophomores," she's telling Sunny. "With that brain of yours, you can handle another elective, I'm sure. Should I sign you up?"

"I was actually asking for my sister," Sunny replies.

The lady's smile fades. "Oh. I'm sorry. Upper division drama classes are reserved for advanced students only—those who have studied drama for three or four years. The teacher is *very* choosy about who qualifies."

A bell rings, and I nudge Sunny with my elbow. "That's fine. Let's go," I say. But she doesn't budge.

"Why can't my sister at least try out for the drama classes?" Sunny's voice and stance suddenly remind me of Ma, which is strange. They look nothing alike.

Baba isn't moving either, his eyes still fixed on my face. I lift my eyes to let him glimpse the desire in mine. *Yes, Baba. This is my dream.* Can he see it? Will he allow it?

The registrar looks from me to Sunny, studying my sister's

stubborn body language for a long minute. "I'll have to talk to the drama teacher—"

"We can wait," Sunny says.

"Please," I add.

The registrar sighs. "Okay, sit over there. I'll call her now. She owes me a favor anyway."

We head to the bench in the lobby, but none of us sit down.

"Theater, my Star?" Baba asks. I listen carefully, but there's no disappointment in his tone, only surprise.

"Yes, Baba," I say. "It's been an interest of mine. And I think I might be good at it. But Ma—"

Baba takes my hand in both of his. "My grandmother used to organize natok in the village for the children—she loved to act. There's nothing wrong with telling a story onstage. It's beautiful work; it brings people together. Rabindranath Tagore wrote plays, didn't he? I'll handle your mother—don't worry about that."

Sunny shoots me a grin. I'm suddenly not in the least bit tired. With Baba on my side, there's nothing stopping me. But first things first—will I get in the class?

The registrar puts down the receiver and gestures for us to return to her desk. I hurry forward with Baba and Sunny right behind me.

"She's agreed to let you audition today in the theater at three o'clock," she tells me. "Don't be late. Ms. Barry is a very busy, passionate woman. I certainly hope you're good, for my sake. I told her you were talented even though I have no idea what you can do."

"She is *extremely* talented," says Sunny. "You won't be sorry."

I manage to return the registrar's smile. I've never auditioned before. Not outside of my fantasies, anyway. But I used to hide in the back of the school theater in London and watch Mrs. Campbell test aspiring actors. What will an American drama teacher ask of me? I can't fail now, not with Sunny pushing for it, not with Baba taking it in both of his hands.

"I'll be back at three to watch your audition," he says before departing. "Mishti, save me a seat in the theater."

The rest of the day goes by in a blur. Nothing affects me—curious stares from classmates, teachers introducing their subjects to other restless seniors, boys who take in my face and figure with appreciative eyes. Baba is coming to my audition! I have to prove to him—and myself—that this dream is worth what it will cost him.

When Sunny and I meet for lunch in the cafeteria, I'm suddenly gripped by fear. "Can I act?" I ask my sister.

"It's like breathing for you," she says, handing me a

sandwich. "You've been acting for years. Just not on a real stage, with a real audience. This is going to be easy."

The theater is vast and empty and smells like new carpeting. Rows and rows of waiting seats are padded in orange and purple plush cushioning. Overhead, complicated lights line the ceiling, ready to obey the stage director. A dozen or so students are chatting at the foot of the stage. The acoustics in this place are so good their conversation reaches all the way to the back.

"Catherine's so good . . . Who's doing costumes this year . . . Are we having a full orchestra . . ."

Slowly, I head down the aisle toward them. Where's my sister? Oh, good. There she is, waving from a row near the middle. Baba's not here yet—maybe Ma's so furious with him he won't show up.

A slender, tall woman with a wispy gray ponytail emerges from backstage. She's wearing a black dress, a white scarf around her neck, and silver bracelets on her wrists. As soon as she sees me, she beckons me forward. "Are you Tara Das? I'm Jocelyn Barry. Come up here, please."

I stride forward, push through the knot of students, and

trot up the stairs to the stage. The students grow quiet, following my every move.

"We don't have much time," Ms. Barry says. "I assume you were told I don't usually accept new seniors?"

I nod and glance over my shoulder. Baba is taking a seat next to Sunny; he's handing her a huge cookie and another Styrofoam cup full of something to drink. Catching my eye, he smiles and lifts his right thumb. I guess that means he's told Ma what's going on. Thank God for new houses and renewed romances.

"Well, let me see what you can do," Ms. Barry says. "Can you sing?"

"I love to sing."

She hands me a script. "We'll be putting this show on this year. It's a musical."

I read the cover page and my heart skips a beat.

It's *West Side Story*.

"Read Maria," Ms. Barry commands. "Scene Three."

I've seen the movie version of the musical three times. Once in London, and then two more times when Jenny and I snuck out of school in Flushing to catch a matinee. I made her stay for the second showing. Rita Moreno took on the role of Anita, and she was fabulous. Passion, energy, beauty—she had it all. She *was* Anita. Natalie Wood starred as Maria. *She isn't* becoming *Maria the way I would*, I remember thinking as I munched on popcorn. And now I'm being given a chance to prove it.

Ms. Barry has been considering the faces of people standing below us. "Catherine, will you come up here and play Anita?"

A willowy girl with long brown hair joins us onstage. She smiles at me as she picks up a copy of the script, but it doesn't reach her eyes.

"You have the first line, Tara," says Ms. Barry.

Baba and Sunny are rooting hard for me; I can feel their love reaching all the way up here. I take a deep breath. *BECOME Maria*, I tell myself.

"And, line," says Ms. Barry.

We start.

I'm in a bridal shop. Anita is transforming a white communion dress into a party dress for me. I hand her a pair of imaginary scissors. "Por favor, Anita. Make the neck *lower!*" My tone is wheedling. I want the dress to make me look like a woman.

"Stop it, Maria."

"One inch. How much can one *little* inch do?" *Oh, to be a woman. To finally look like a woman.*

"Too much."

I'm exasperated. "Anita, it is now to be a dress of dancing, no longer for kneeling in front of an altar."

"With those boys you can start in dancing and end up kneeling."

The dialogue keeps going.

I know some of the lines by heart, but Catherine has the whole thing memorized.

We finish the scene.

Tara returns inside my skin. Catherine becomes Catherine again, and she's not smiling anymore.

There's a silence.

And then someone starts applauding in the back. I think it might be Baba, or Sunny, but I'm not sure. The small audience in front joins in.

Ms. Barry is studying my face. "Have you acted before?"

I tell the truth: "I've been acting ever since I can remember. But never onstage."

"Are you willing to work hard?"

"Very."

"Okay, then. Welcome to Ridgeford High School's drama program. For now, you'll understudy for Catherine in the lead role of Maria. But if you're the kind to learn quickly, we'll see what happens as we get closer to the actual performance dates. You're both busy seniors, so I'm sure she'll be glad to share the load. Right, Catherine? Why don't you fill Tara in on our class schedule?"

I know Catherine isn't completely glad, but she's an actor, too. "Welcome, Tara," she says coolly. "Upper-division drama is second period, every day, and we rehearse after school three days a week. Monday, Wednesday, Friday."

"I'll be here," I say. "And thanks for giving me the chance, Ms. Barry."

"We're starting rehearsals right now. If you're in, you stay," Ms. Barry says. Then she claps her hands together twice, hard. "Let's go, people. Time is short."

The other students join us onstage. In the empty theater, Baba and Sunny stand up to gather their belongings. My sister flashes two fingers in a peace-sign goodbye. "Tell them what 'Tara' means!" Baba calls out in English.

"Your father?" Ms. Barry asks, smiling for the first time.

"And my sister."

"So what *does* your name mean?" Catherine asks.

"Star." I don't hesitate. "It means star."

2
Travelers
1976–81

Sonia

A Daughter for Life

"Such a tragedy."

"Horrible. Heartbreaking."

Big Harm and her husband, our old neighbors in Flushing, have driven to Ridgeford for Baba's shradh ceremony. "He'd just gotten another big promotion, did you hear? And now . . ."

"What do you think she'll do?"

"Return to Calcutta, I suppose. A widow with two girls to marry off? She doesn't really have a choice, does she?"

Through the swinging half door that leads into the kitchen, I overhear snippets of conversation from the dining room. *Pretend he's in Ghana. He's in India, visiting relatives.*

Each time people talk about what happened, I've been reciting imaginary travels for Baba in my head. Today, my mantra is taking a lot of effort; I can hardly wait until these guests leave.

We can't get started until the purohit gets here. Wearing a dhoti and a saffron-colored scarf draped around his shoulders, the high-caste Hindu priest had accompanied us to the crematorium. He'd performed the ceremonies and rituals perfectly, according to Big Harm. He'd asked Big Harm's husband, who shares the Das surname because he's some sort of relative, to snip a lock of Baba's hair and put it in the urn before . . .

Well, anyway, that was two weeks ago. As soon as the priest gets here today, the shradh ceremony can start.

"Why is he so late?" I ask Starry.

"I'm not sure what's keeping him," my sister answers. "He charges a big enough fee."

We're both wearing salwar kameez outfits that smell like mothballs. Ma is draped in one of the white widow's saris our grandmother sent from Calcutta. Starry starts arranging store-bought shortbread cookies on a platter. "How many people are out there?" she asks.

"Too many," I answer. "Can't you hear them? They've eaten almost all the roshogollas and shondesh already."

Starry hands me the platter. "Pass these around, Sunny. Good thing one of the aunties brought a boatload of payesh. I'll heat that up now."

"Let me stay in here. You take these cookies."

"Oh, all right."

I start stirring the sweet, milky rice pudding while Starry backs out of the swinging door. Ma is lighting an incense stick at the small altar of statues tucked in an alcove behind the kitchen counter. She looks up, eyes swollen with grief, but doesn't speak. She hasn't said anything since that day in the hospital. After the doctor pulled back the sheet, she said his name to identify his body: "Rajeev Das."

It was the first time we'd heard her say his name. He always called her "Ranee," but wives aren't supposed to call their husbands by proper names. "Husband," Ma always said—or "Apni," the honorific "you," or "Tumi," the familiar "you," if she didn't think we could overhear. If Bengali wives follow the good-wife rules, they supposedly bless their husbands with long life and prosperity. But it hadn't worked for Ma.

It worries me that I haven't cried yet. No tears come, even though my eyes sting like I'm walking through smoke. I can't read. I can't even write. I don't feel anything, so what's the use? I don't even try to provoke Ma into speaking. *What's the point of lighting incense?* I could ask her now. *All those offerings you've made for the Das family, to Saraswati, goddess of education. Lakshmi, goddess of wealth. Maybe you shouldn't have given the biggest plate of fruit to Kali, goddess of destruction. Maybe* she's *the one to blame.*

But Ma won't fight back. She weeps and sobs through the night, but she hasn't spoken. Nothing other than muttering in front of those goddesses. Baba never prayed to statues. He believed in a loving Creator, the maker of life. After we moved to Ridgeford, he'd ride his bicycle to a park along the bluffs and watch the sunset to "meditate on God's splendor," as he liked to say. I joined him when I could, jogging while he slowed down so I could keep pace. He'd point out the symmetric perfection of a butterfly, the sunlight shimmering on the river, and the delicate aroma of a yellow rose.

"These were not made randomly, Mishti," he used to tell me. "A mathematical Mind, the greatest Mind of all, a Mind full of perfection and love—this type of Mind is behind all of creation."

I ladle the payesh into small glass dishes our parents found in a secondhand shop. *How wrong he was. A God of perfection and love would never have allowed the accident.* The nights are the worst. I try not to imagine the agony he must have endured: limbs, organs, and bicycle mangled by a hit-and-run driver. Dying alone by the side of the road before the paramedics could reach him.

He's in Malaysia on a work trip. He's in New Delhi. He'll be home soon.

Starry pops her head into the kitchen. "The priest is sick, so he sent his son. At least, I think he's the priest's son. He looks more like a flower child—I think he's twenty-five at the most. Bring the payesh. Come, Ma."

I carry the tray of payesh behind my mother and sister. Countless pairs of sandals and chappals are strewn around the entry. In the living room, about thirty or so Bengalis have taken their seats. The younger ones are standing or sitting on the floor. Hands reach for the payesh as I lower the tray. Other hands are still passing the platter of cookies around.

Sitting cross-legged on the hearth is a young man with a ponytail. He's wearing blue jeans, a kurta, and a saffron scarf draped around his neck—and is smiling as if he's about to officiate a wedding instead of a shradh ceremony. He's bearded, his kurta is unbuttoned, and three gold disco chains adorn his hairy chest.

Starry leads Ma to him. "Ma, this is Mohan, the son of the purohit," she says.

The flower child gives Ma a half-hearted Namaste. "I'm, er, sorry for your loss, Auntie. I'm also sorry my father got dysentery. My mother tries, but her cooking isn't perfect. So he sent me in his place. I'll try my best, I promise." He's speaking English, and his accent is almost 100 percent American, like Starry's. I've been told that you can still hear some BBC in mine, even after three years.

Big Harm and two other women are sitting on the sofa closest to the fireplace. Big Harm, whose girth has grown since we left Flushing, doesn't budge, but the others shift to make room for Ma. Ma says nothing as she takes her seat.

A large framed photo adorned with garlands stands on the mantel over the fireplace. Beside it is an aluminum urn. I can't look at either of them. Instead, I place the empty tray on the coffee table, and sit next to Starry at Ma's feet.

I'm right across from Mohan, and there's a strange smell coming from him, like . . . Is that *marijuana*?

"Where are the, you know, the remains?" he asks, still using English.

Without looking up, Starry gestures toward the urn on the mantel. "Up there."

"Oh, there he is! Wonderful!"

It sounds like he's spotted a long-lost friend.

Mohan scans the unsmiling faces around the room and realizes he might have made a mistake. "Are you going to take him . . . er, take them to India and put them into the Ganges River? That's the thing to do, right?"

"Yes, young man, that is exactly what we do," answers Big Harm in Bangla, frowning at him from the sofa. She turns to Ma. "Obviously his father hasn't trained him properly. I'm so sorry, Ranee."

"Don't worry, Aunties," Mohan says. "We'll get this done one way or another. We're all learning here, aren't we?"

Big Harm continues as if Mohan hadn't spoken. "About those ashes—they need to be discarded properly. A nephew on your husband's side must empty the urn. You and the girls will be returning to live in Calcutta soon, Ranee, I suppose? I've heard you can take ashes with you on the plane if you fill in the right forms."

Our mother doesn't answer the question.

Mohan begins riffling through the pages of a book called *Vedic Rituals for English Speakers*. "Birth rites, wedding blessings . . . Ah! Here we are. Death rituals." He mutters a few sentences to himself. "Oh, yes, this is it. Fifteen days after death. Prayers. Oldest son shaves head and recites after priest." He looks up. "Well, here's the priest. But where's the son?"

There's a silence.

"He had no son, you—" Big Harm says. She stops herself in time, but everyone else in the room fills in the blank: *idiot!*

Everyone, that is, except Mohan. "What a lucky, lucky man he is—er, was," he says, still obliviously hearty. "You know what they say—*a daughter's a daughter for life, but a son's only a son until he takes a wife.* Or something like that. Anyway, he's got two daughters, right? Why can't one of them recite the prayers with me?"

Yes. Why can't we? Suddenly, I like this young, hip version of a purohit.

Big Harm gestures at her husband and Little Harm stands up. "Did your father teach you nothing?" he asks. "In India, only a son can perform funeral rites for his father."

"Oh, right," says Mohan. "Forgot that rule. Doesn't make much sense, though, here, does it? I mean, it's 1976, people. And we're in America, right?"

Little Harm is making his way to the mantel, frowning and shaking his head. "If there's no son, the job goes to the closest male relative in the Das family line. Since we're so far from the nephews in Calcutta, I'll recite the prayers after you. But can you even read Sanskrit?"

"No worries there. My father translated, I mean transcribed—wait, is it transliterated? Yes, that's the one where you use English letters to make the Sanskrit words, right?"

Little Harm gestures impatiently at Starry to move so he can take her place. Suddenly, fury blazes through me. At the crematorium, I had been too numb to notice Little Harm taking his big role, but I'm not going to let him do the shradh, too. Besides finding him that first apartment, what did this man and his wife ever do for Baba?

I gather my courage and look up at my father's portrait. *A daughter's a daughter for life, Baba,* I tell him. Then I stand up, grab Starry's hand, and pull my sister to her feet. "My sister and I will return in a few minutes," I announce. "And then we will start the shradh."

A buzz travels through the room, but when Ma doesn't protest or scold me, the crowd parts for us. I pull my sister through the entry, up the stairs, and into our parents' bathroom. "Find the scissors, Starry," I say.

"Why? What are you doing, Sunny? You're embarrassing us."

"So what? Baba doesn't need a son. He has us, doesn't he?"

Starry looks into the mirror where our father used to shave every morning. She puts her arm around me. "You're right. He does. And he always will. I'm the oldest, Sunny. I'll do it."

"No chance," I say. "It was my idea. Besides, the same people who made up the son rule probably made up the old-est child rule. Let's break both at the same time. Come on, we have to hurry."

An electric razor is still charging near our parents' tooth-brushes. Starry hunts in a drawer and finds a pair of shears.

"Girls? Are you coming?" It's Big Harm, calling from downstairs.

"Be there soon!" Starry yells through the door.

I stand on a towel while she lops off my curls with quick snaps of the shears. My head feels lighter without them. Then, while I lean over the sink, my sister arcs the razor from the nape of my skull to the top of my forehead, again and again, one row at a time. I try not to move, but it feels like she's slicing instead of shaving me.

"What's taking so long? Everything okay up there?" This time it's one of the "uncles"; I don't recognize the voice.

"We're coming!"

Hand in hand, we descend the stairs. When my head comes into sight, a gasp ricochets through the living room. Ma cries out, jolted into words at last: "Baby! Ma! What have you done?"

"I'll be reciting the prayers for Baba," I say, shocking the entire room into silence. I've said it in Bangla, so there's no doubt about my meaning.

Starry and I make our way back to the mantel. We settle again into our cross-legged positions at Ma's feet, facing the young priest. Little Harm throws a look at his wife, but gets up and moves back to his seat.

"I like your head, kid," Mohan says to me.

"Thanks," I answer.

"What about you?" he asks my sister.

It's Starry's turn to look up at the portrait and urn on the mantel. "I promise to empty that urn into the Ganges," she answers.

Ma's hands reach over to stroke my skull and pat Starry's cheek. Then she stands and turns to face the room. "My daughters and I will stay in America," she says. "In this house that their father bought. Please let the prayers begin for his soul."

The flower child of a priest smiles at her. "Groovy, Auntie."

Ma takes her seat again, and this time Big Harm moves over to make more room. Mohan opens his book and starts reciting the transliterated words. Bowing my shaved head in front of my father's portrait, I repeat the age-old Bangla prayers in a strong and steady voice.

Sonia

Liberation

I PULL A TACK OUT OF THE SMALL BOX AND push it through the poster on the bulletin board. JOIN THE EQUAL RIGHTS CLUB! announce the red letters. I've been the founding president of the ERC chapter at Ridgeford High for two years, but so far we only have two members: me and my best friend, Sahara.

"When and where's this women's lib meeting?" drawls an unfamiliar voice behind me.

I turn, ready to give my usual spiel—Monday afternoons in the art room, we cover all kinds of justice and gender issues, blah, blah, blah. To my surprise, it's a guy wearing a football jersey. The voice belongs to Lou Johnson, the starting running back on the high school varsity team. He moved to Ridgeford this year from somewhere in the South and turned the team around. He's one of only two black players. "Black Lightning," they call him. Tall and lean, with terra-cotta eyes that make his face look even darker.

Handsome and knows it, I think, and keep my tone extra-cool: "It's right there on the poster. Monday afternoons. In the art room. You can read, right?"

The jock grins. "Is that warm welcome for everybody, or just me?"

I don't answer. Instead, I move into my silence-is-power body language: feet apart, fists on hips, frown on face. But his eyes seem to be hunting for the curves I keep hidden under one of Baba's old shirts. For seventeen years, I've never wanted to be seen by guys. It's easier to escape the patriarchy when male eyes don't notice you. And now this guy is *seeing* me all right, taking in every inch of me with that earthy, bold gaze. Silence-is-power stance number two: cross flexed arms across body, narrow eyes.

"I'm all for the liberation of women," he says. "Can I come and join y'all?"

He's not very good at reading nonverbals. But at least his words are respectful. "Are you a feminist?" I ask.

"I'm trying to become one," he says. "I like to think that

some of my vases are feminist. Have you seen them? They're on display in the art room. You know, where your club meets."

I almost drop the box of tacks and a few skitter to the floor. *This* is the student who sculpted those curvy, heavy ceramic containers? I stayed after club last Monday to admire their weight and shape.

I bend over to retrieve the tacks, but he does, too, and our heads crash. "Ouch," I say, rubbing my scalp. My hair has grown back since Starry shaved it, but I keep it short now. I like the style, but it's not as good of a buffer as my curls used to be.

"Sorry," he says, handing me three tacks.

To my relief, I see Sahara strolling over, her trademark warm smile in place. When the news spread about Baba's death, most of my classmates handled me like I was made of glass. Sahara, though, stuck even closer to me than before.

Now she throws her arms around this fake-feminist jock who's making me even more nervous than I already am. *Traitor.* "Congratulations, Lou! I just heard the news. I've been so excited for Sonia I forgot our school has two winners."

Great. I'd been wondering about the other winner of the essay contest. And here he is. "But you're not in Honors French," I can't help saying.

Sahara's beaded braids dance around her round face.

"Lou doesn't need to be, Sunny. He's already fluent. Are you guys ready for the assembly? There's the bell now."

A stream of students begins to head toward the auditorium. "See you onstage, Sonia," says Lou. "Bye, Sahara."

"What's up, Sunny?" asks Sahara. "Lou's a sweetie. You were kind of rude."

"I don't know. I can't believe I have to travel with that guy."

Sahara smiles. "You'll be fine. Lou's cool. Come on, let's get in there. We don't want to be late."

I follow her into the auditorium, and we choose two empty seats near an aisle. I'll have to go up there soon, in front of all those eyes. To them, the tragedy happened a while ago. I should be moving on, growing my curls back, being social again. But it doesn't seem like that to me. To me, it's been an hour. A minute.

"You never used to be judgy," Sahara tells me gently, her eyes on my face. "Feisty, yes. Sometimes even prickly. But never rude. Before the accident, you were—"

I stiffen. "You know I don't want to talk about that, Sahara. Not here."

"When, then? Where?"

Sahara's tone is insistent, and a girl beside us gives us a curious look. "Shhhh . . ." I say.

"Don't shush me," says Sahara, but she lowers her voice. "It's been six months already, and you still won't talk about it. Not even with me. You won't even write about it."

"I can't, Sahara," I whisper. "Not yet."

"Isn't there anything I can do? You never laugh anymore. Remember how we used to lose it during gym class when both of us stunk so badly—at every sport? And I don't think you've even cried yet. Have you?"

I don't answer, but Sahara's right. I didn't cry, not even in the hospital. A door locked somewhere inside me that day and I can't find the key. If there is one.

Sahara is shaking her head, making the beads dance again. "I keep asking Jesus to help you, but He's taking His sweet time."

I roll my eyes. The only thing wrong with Sahara is that she's crazy religious. "He's busy helping all the white men in the world," I answer. "He'll get to me one day."

Sure enough, Sahara takes the bait. "Stop right there, Sonia Das. *My* Jesus is a brown-skinned carpenter who *loves* women. I know He's going to answer my prayers for you soon."

Principal Matthews is walking up to the podium. "Then stop talking and start praying," I tell my friend. "It's almost time. I'm so nervous."

"I have some exciting news, students," Principal Matthews says. "Most of you know about the Francophone Foundation's annual essay competition. The topic is always the same: 'My French Heritage.' The Foundation sends six high school seniors in New Jersey to Paris for a week in the spring. All expenses paid. And this year, not one, but *two* of the winners are from Ridgeford High."

A low murmur spreads through the room. Only a few of us know who the winners are, and Dr. Matthews is building the suspense. "Round-trip tickets," she says. "Hotel. Meals. The Eiffel Tower. The Arc de Triomphe. Fashion. Culture. Food. History. All in the City of Light. *Paris.*"

I'm feeling light-headed as I wait for the principal to announce my name. I still can't believe I won. It feels like a long time since something good has happened. And this is more than good; it's exactly what I need. A week in Paris, escaping everything that reminds me of—

"Ladies and gentlemen, may I present our winners? Come up here, Ms. Sonia Das and Mr. Lou Johnson!"

The room explodes into cheering. Lou stands up five rows in front of us, and I can see his football buddies slapping various parts of his anatomy. Sahara gives my hand a squeeze. Lou waits in the aisle for me and steps back to let me go first. I brush past him and lead the way to the stage, trying to hide my nerves. Somehow I make it to the podium and glance across a blurry sea of faces, trying desperately to find Sahara's familiar one. She's easy to spot; the audience in this school is mostly white. Black Lightning and I must look quite the sight as we flank the principal.

Dr. Matthews taps the mike and the crowd settles down. "I'll be interviewing both of our winners. Let's start with Sonia, shall we? Have you traveled much, Sonia?"

Good. An easy question. "Yes. My whole life."

"How old were you when you came to the United States? To New York, right? And where did you live before that?"

I'd rehearsed my answers in Dr. Matthews's office, but now I had to concentrate to keep them straight. "I was fifteen. Yes, New York. But we lived in London before that, and briefly in Ghana. And first in India, where I was born."

Lou is leaning forward at the principal's other side, his dusty eyes focused on me.

"Have *you* traveled much, Lou?" Dr. Matthews asks, tipping the microphone over to him.

"I've not been to France, ma'am," he answers. "But Louisiana—which shares my name, Louis—is a very French state."

Dr. Matthews nods. "That's what your essay is about, right?"

"Yes, ma'am."

"Tell us more, Lou."

"My family's been in Louisiana for decades and my mother has French blood, believe it or not. My skin might look like coffee-no-cream, but I've got some au lait in here somewhere." He smiles, and the audience laughs with him. His pronunciation of the French phrase is decent, I notice.

"And what was the focus of your essay?"

"It was about our faith, ma'am. We're Catholic, thanks mostly to the French part of us. Even one of the most violent, bloody antireligious revolutions in history couldn't keep the French away from the Church."

The principal turns back to me. "And what was your essay about, Sonia?"

I catch Lou's eye across the podium and take it as a challenge. Reaching for the mike, I angle it toward me again. "I wrote about liberty, fraternity, equality. The three themes of the French Revolution, which I see as one of the greatest events in history." I emphasize the word "greatest" and look across at Lou again.

"But how did you relate the French Revolution to your own life, Sonia?" Dr. Matthews asks. "I'm sure we're all intrigued by how a person born in India can claim a French heritage."

I'm relaxing now, enjoying the freedom to talk about one of my favorite topics. "People in Africa, Asia, and Latin America have a two-sided heritage from Europe. We have a heritage of oppression from the years they colonized us, but we also have a heritage of freedom." My voice gets stronger, bolder, as I remember the research I did for my essay. "One hundred and fifty years after France's revolution, India finally took hold of the great European ideas about democracy, threw off British rule, and became a free country governed by the people. That's what I wrote about."

I can hear the audience shuffling and muttering. I've gone on too long. Someone in the front yawns audibly, and Dr. Matthews frowns at him. "Thank you, Lou and Sonia!" she says. "Ridgeford High is very proud of our winning team. We'll be eager to interview you again when you return from your week in France."

As the applause begins once more, Lou stands back to let me descend the stage first. I sense the restored attention of an audience that's more interested in what they see than in what they've heard. Two of the handful of brown kids in the school, heading off to Paris together. Lou: tall, lean, relaxed, wearing jeans and that football jersey—popular with the whole school already, even though he's new. Me: stocky, intense, short hair, stud earrings, wearing a man's shirt and baggy jeans—the girl with the dead dad, friends with only one person after two and a half years in this town.

I slip back into my seat beside Sahara.

"You did great," she tells me.

"Thanks. Wish you were coming instead of him. What's that word we learned in English? You know, when two complete opposites are stuck together? Like 'jumbo shrimp'?"

"An oxymoron?"

"That's us," I say. "Louisiana Johnson and Sonia Das. The winning oxymoron from Ridgeford High."

"An oxymoron makes a new meaning out of two opposites, Sunny."

"Not this time."

A voice calls from the hall outside my bedroom. "Mishti!"

My eyes fly open at the familiar nickname. "Baba?" I answer softly, still half asleep.

My sister's head pops in the door. "You'd better get ready. Ma's making breakfast. I'll help you take your suitcase down once you're dressed."

Her head disappears, and I take deep breaths, fending off the sharp stab of pain that comes with every awakening. I wonder why Starry used Baba's nickname for me. "Mishti," or "Sweetie," is what *he* used to call me. *Mishti! Come see this bird! Come quickly! You'll miss it!* His voice is so clear in my head.

Pretend he's in Ghana, I tell myself. *He's in Malaysia. He'll be back soon.*

It must have been a slip of the tongue, because Starry would never hurt me. Not on purpose, anyway. She must be missing him more than she lets on, even though she keeps so busy with studies and performances. But Starry's grieving hard, too. She eats more than she used to, and dresses differently, like she doesn't really care about attention. Plus, she's stopped singing completely—unless it's a song for a rehearsal or audition.

Last year, she won a scholarship to Manhattan's Academy of Theater Arts, thanks to a brilliant audition and a raving recommendation from her Ridgeford High drama teacher. Now she takes the train to Manhattan every morning and comes home late in the evening. Meanwhile, I'm counting the days until I graduate and head off to college. I can't wait to leave this sad house, with a ghost of a mother wandering from room to room in her white widow's sari.

I pick up the new notebook that Starry gave me yesterday. That gift, too, reminds me of Baba. Sahara was right; I haven't written a word in six months. Is it any use taking it

with me? I sigh, tuck it into my satchel, and haul my suitcase down the stairs.

Familiar smells fill the house—sandalwood, turmeric, bay
leaves, incense, black pepper. Ma is frying luchi at the stove.
Already, a pile of the light, round, puffy bread waits on the
table. She hasn't made luchi since Baba—

Starry sits down. "Is that egg-and-potato curry, Ma?"
she asks.

Our mother's wearing white—as she has for the last six
months—no makeup, no jewelry, eating no meat or fish. She's
keeping Bengali restrictions even though we're thousands
of miles from India. Which means she stays inside most of
the time. In the olden days, widows used to throw themselves
on their dead husbands' burning pyres—or were thrown.
Disgusting. But isn't that what Ma is doing, too? Symboli-
cally, anyway. Starry lectures me to be kind, but I can't help
wanting to yank Ma out of her patriarchal prison.

Now my sister throws me another "be nice" look.

"Smells great, Ma," I manage. "Thank you."

"Nothing but the best for my smart girl," Ma says. "But
what does this school think, sending children like you alone
to a foreign country?"

Now that *sounds a little like the old Ma.* I've been worrying about her lack of protest or questioning about this trip

since I won the contest. "I'm seventeen, Ma," I say. "And I'm not going alone. Another student from Ridgeford High is joining me, remember? And four others from all around the state."

"Stay close to that girl from your school," Ma warns. "Don't wander off by yourself like you always do."

He's no girl, I think, picturing the lean, dark lines of Lou.

Starry throws me a "shut up" look. Ever since she found out about Lou, she's been warning me not to tell Ma about him. "She doesn't need to know you're traveling with a guy. And especially not a black guy," she says when we're alone. My sister even suggested that I shouldn't invite Sahara over. "You can't get her fired up about stuff like that anymore," Starry lectures. "Not for a while, at least. She's fragile. I see it in her eyes." Reluctantly, I agreed, but I have reasons of my own. I know Sahara probably wonders why we always go to her house instead of mine, but she never asks. I don't bring it up, either—the reasons are too complicated to explain, even to my best friend.

Ma lifts the simmering curry from the stove and heaps huge servings on two plates. "Eat quickly, girls. Are you sure you can drive the car all the way to the airport?"

Baba taught both of us to drive and took us to get our

licenses. I can't help glancing at the empty fourth chair. *He's in Ghana. India. Singapore.*

"Yes, Ma, I'm sure," Starry answers. "Why don't you come along? That way I'll have company on the way home."

"No. I'll say goodbye here."

Surprise, surprise. The widow's prison.

After breakfast, I head to the landing, where Baba's portrait is displayed. Ma keeps it adorned with garlands of fresh flowers. I stand there for a few minutes, memorizing his face all over again, until a gentle hand taps my shoulder. "Ready, Sunny?" my sister asks. She's lugging my suitcase. Ma is standing beside Starry, wiping her eyes with the end of her sari.

While Starry loads my suitcase into the Chevy Nova, Ma strokes my short hair. "I wish you'd grow it back, Baby. I miss your curls."

To my surprise, she kisses my cheek before retreating into the house. Baba was the affectionate one in the family; Ma never hugged or kissed us much, even before the accident. This unexpected kiss feels like a bon voyage blessing from *both* of my parents.

At Newark International Airport, my sister and I find the check-in counter for the plane to Paris. A slim, sophisticated-looking woman approaches us holding a sign with six names on it. I see Lou's name written under mine, but he's nowhere in sight. She introduces herself as Dr. Margot, the Francophone Foundation chaperone for the trip, and helps me check in. My Indian passport makes the process more complicated.

"Can't wait to become a citizen," I mutter to Starry. Baba used to talk about the three of us going to the swearing-in ceremony at City Hall. Now it would just be Starry and me. No chance of Ma joining us. *I'll die an Indian*, she always says.

"Two more years until we can apply," Starry says. "Hard to believe it's only been three since we left London."

I know she's remembering the last time we were at this airport. So am I.

Starry walks me to the foot of the escalator leading to the departure gates.

"Let's say goodbye here," I say.

"I'll be waiting outside customs when you come home."

She reaches for my right hand and clasps it inside both of hers. Hers are smaller than Baba's, but the pressure and warmth on my skin feels so familiar. She lets go, and the escalator draws me up and away until my waving sister disappears. Now I'm really on my own. I take a deep breath, step off the escalator, and head to the departure gate.

The Francophone Foundation has splurged on accommodations for the prize winners. They've reserved two rooms for the week at the Saint James Paris, an exclusive château hotel. The boys are going to be in one room and the three of us girls will share the other.

We head upstairs with our suitcases. My roommates are cordial, but they're best friends from the same school, so they make it obvious they plan to spend this week together. They pounce on the double bed; I claim the single rollaway.

"See you in half an hour, Sonia," one says.

"We'll be in the lobby having coffee," the other adds.

I unpack after they leave, enjoying the solitude and luxury of the room. I finger the thick toweled robes, read the labels on the amenities, pat the eiderdown quilts, inspect the well-stocked refrigerator, and step into the huge, empty, gleaming bathtub. After a refreshing hot shower, I put on clean clothes—jeans, dangly peace-sign earrings, and a T-shirt featuring Gloria Steinem's face—and head down to meet the rest of the group.

In the lobby, Dr. Margot hands out schedules and maps. It's morning in France, and we have the whole day ahead to start exploring Paris. The French attitude toward seventeen- and eighteen-year-olds, she informs us, is quite different from the American one. There will be no "policing" of students our age. We're to follow our own interests during the days. In the evenings, the Foundation has organized lectures, discussions, and excursions to the opera and the ballet.

"Paris is a very manageable city. The only requirement I have for you is that you pick a partner and stay together." She surveys the six of us over her reading glasses before going back to her clipboard. "Here are museum passes, metro tickets, pocket money, and the Foundation's emergency phone number. Meet back here at seven for dinner and the first evening session. Any questions?"

There aren't any. She distributes the goodies and strides off. I guess she meant what she said about giving us freedom. My roommates turn to each other and begin discussing their plans. The two other boys, classmates in a Manhattan prep school, exit the lobby together.

That leaves Lou and me.

"Shall we?" he asks.

I notice he's clean-shaven and that his hair is newly trimmed and shaped. I have to admit it looks nice, but I'm not going to tell him that. "Your hairstyle looks like mine," I say instead.

He smiles. "Don't think I could pull off those earrings, though."

You probably could, I think. He's wearing jeans, too, and a colorful unisex African-style caftan. It reminds me suddenly of Ghana. I can still remember some Twi: Eti sen? *How are you?*

"I can't seem to remember much French since we got off the plane," I say, changing the subject. I ease my shoulders into my backpack as we walk toward the doors. "Maybe it's jet lag. Are you really fluent?"

"I hope so. My grandparents are, anyway. Where should we go first?"

We decide to climb the Eiffel Tower—what a view! "Literally breathtaking," I say at the top. Lou, though, is quiet, his eyes taking in everything. Back on the ground, we stroll along the quays bordering the Seine, where so many writers walked for centuries before penning their masterpieces. I tell Lou about some of my modern-day French heroes, feminist writers like Chantal Chawaf, Hélène Cixous, and Luce Irigaray.

"Do you want to write novels or nonfiction?" he asks.

"I love reading fiction to escape," I say. "But when I write,

I like getting deeper into the issues and thinking critically about them. I love argument. So, nonfiction, I guess."

"Novels change hearts, though. *And* minds."

We discuss this back and forth, and I hardly notice the boats spinning along the river, or the people pushing past us. Finally, we stop for a coffee in a sidewalk café. Lou uses his hands when he talks, long fingers carving the air into shapes that match his words. "My mother teaches drama at the Ridgeford Community Center," he tells me. "Still gets a part on Broadway every now and then."

"That's what my sister wants to do!" I say as we settle into two seats near the street.

"Maybe I can introduce her to Mom when we get back."

The waiter gives us menus and Lou looks his over while I try to imagine bringing him home, introducing him to Starry and Ma. Despite the mostly white neighborhood Ma moved us to, my best friend is black. I agreed not to ask Sahara to come over, but not because Starry talks about Ma's "fragility." My reason is different: I don't trust Ma to welcome my best friend. And Sahara's a *girl*. If I brought a black *boy* into our living room, Ma might shatter altogether. Or explode. *Maybe it would shock her back to life, like those paddles they use in emergency rooms.*

We order espressos and croissants. "We'd better introduce

them soon, though," Lou says. "I'm the youngest, and my parents are moving to Harlem after I graduate. Mom got an offer to teach at some exclusive private school in Manhattan."

"What about your father?"

"He's a sociology professor at Princeton. I figure Dad and I can commute together. There's free tuition at Princeton if I get in. My brother's there now, studying math. They've got a pretty good art program, too."

"You'll get in. Faculty kid and all." I feel a twinge of nervousness. "I'm applying there, too. Their English department is outstanding."

"How'd you do on those crazy college tests? Sahara told me you and I have the same GPA."

Sahara. Sharing my personal information! What are you up to, girl? I've never met a guy who rivals me in grades. At this rate, Lou and I will be vying to give the school's valedictorian speech in June.

I'm embarrassed to share my super-high SAT scores, but I'm curious to find out his, so I do.

"You scored better than I did in the verbal part," he says. "But I got twenty points higher than you in math. Sculpting makes me do calculus without even thinking about it." He gestures to the waiter for the bill. "Let's head out. I want to check out that sculpture exhibit in the park we passed, okay?"

We wander slowly through the garden and the sculptures, and he concentrates fiercely on one or two—a glass vase covered in tiny mosaic tiles, and a large stone piece featuring three dancers leaning on each other as they balance on strong feet. He pulls out a camera and starts snapping photos. For some reason, I keep focusing on his long, elegant fingers. And artist's hands. Every now and then, except for when a piece of art is captivating him, I catch him watching me, too. At first his eyes make me uncomfortable, but after a while I let him look. He's not rude. Or pushy, like Gerald was at first. It's almost like he's enjoying the design of me, the same way he appreciates the interlaced ballerinas.

Both of us are trying not to stare at the Parisians. Willowy women wearing tailored blazers stride by with silk scarves cleverly draped around their necks. Cigarettes dangle from manicured fingers; tiny dogs wait patiently for owners to finish espressos; every female foot is shod in a high-heeled designer shoe. A family strolls by: father, mother, two little girls. My stomach clenches as I watch the girls take their father's hands to cross the busy street.

"Ready for the Louvre?" Lou asks after a while. Then, with that easy, handsome grin of his, he adds, "Got a museum named after me, too."

I can't help but smile at that.

Despite the crowds, we line up to catch a glimpse of the Mona Lisa. People are clustering ten deep around it, waiting for a turn to press close to the glass that protects it. But to the left of Leonardo Da Vinci's famous picture, another painting glows with rich colors. Nobody is standing in front of it, so I walk forward to get a closer look.

Inside the lavish gilt frame, a crowd of men surrounds a woman. One of them tugs the woman by her long braid, and the rest lean forward, eyes leering to catch her reactions. The woman clutches a green sheet around her body as she looks down at her feet. I study her expression and decide it's a combination of fear and shame. And hopelessness. I can tell that this woman has lost all hope of freedom.

But a man is walking into the center of the painting with one hand upraised. The crowd has parted to let him through, and they seem to be demanding a reaction from him. I'm suddenly curious to know what happens next. I read the words beside the painting to see if I can find a clue. *"Le Christ et la femme adultère,"* I read. The sign says the painting was done by Lorenzo Lotto in the sixteenth century.

Lou has come up to stand beside me. "I know this story," he says.

"You do? How?"

"Eighteen years of church. A few things had to stick, right? Actually, this is one of my favorites."

"What's going on?"

"They're about to stone the woman for committing adultery."

"And do they?"

"No, ma'am, they do not. They ask him to condemn her, but he bends down and writes something in the dirt. Diverts them. Defuses the situation. De-escalation, I think it's called, when crowd scenes get violent. Then he stands up and looks at them all. 'He who is without sin,' he says, 'let him throw the first stone.' One by one, they all leave."

"What happens to her?"

" 'Where are your accusers?' he asks. 'All of them are gone,' she answers. 'Then neither do I condemn you,' he says. 'Go and sin no more.' "

I gaze at the painting again. "She's about to be free, then," I say quietly, wishing I could see the woman's face again, after the fear and shame left it.

We stroll through the gardens outside the museum. Fountains splash nearby, and the scent of honeysuckle drifts through the air. Lou stops to watch artists at work, and I join him, observing his reactions as he studies each canvas. I'm starting to tell when he likes a piece; I can see it in his eyes.

Only one artist is wearing what I consider a French painter's uniform—black beret, a white blouse with billowing sleeves, and a black scarf. Beside him, a bottle of red wine and a baguette are spread on a checkered cloth. He paints passionately, with huge, violent sweeps, squinting at the soft, muted colors in the sky.

We study his work. Brown and black splotches are scattered across the canvas in a haphazard design. *I don't get it.* My eyes drift back to the soft hues of sunset in the real sky. Suddenly, a flock of pigeons rise squawking from the grass. One of the birds pauses and hovers over the painter, as though it were aiming. Then it releases a glob of white poop that lands neatly in the middle of the canvas's gloomy scene.

"AAAAARRRGH!" bellows the painter. "Bird crap! What's next in this godforsaken country?"

He's an American. Of course. Muttering obscenities, he tries to dab off the white spots. Soon, though, he stops and begins scrutinizing the canvas again. Lou and I watch in amazement.

Then: "Oui! Très jolie! Oh, oui, oui!" the artist moans, becoming more French by the minute. With elaborate sweeps of his brush and huge sighs of satisfaction, he begins to blend the bird's contribution across his canvas.

I look at Lou. Lou looks at me. Later, we won't be able to remember who laughed first.

We collapse on a bench, leaning against each other, snorting and gasping. When we finally manage to stop, I feel a curious sensation of lightness. As if something trapped inside has managed to escape.

It's the first time I've laughed in six months.

When I get back to the hotel room that night, my roommates aren't there yet. I pull out the notebook that Starry gave me and hold it in my hands for a few minutes. Maybe it's time. I pick up a pen. *I miss you, Baba, I miss you*, I write. *Let me tell you what I did today . . .* I start to describe the Eiffel Tower for him, the sculptures, the painting in the Louvre, and even the scene where Lou and I laughed. *You'd like him, Baba. He's easy to be with. Like you.*

The next few days fly by, and now I take my satchel and notebook along with me. Lou doesn't mind when I escape into a corner of a museum or café to write. Staying in the vicinity so we don't get separated, he gives me space and time to scribble the words that are starting to flow again from my pen. I'm making this journal a letter to Baba, writing as though he'll be waiting for me with open arms at the airport.

I tell him what I'm seeing, doing, eating, drinking in Paris, and more about Lou, who is charming, kind, and—there's no denying it—physically beautiful. While I write, Lou sketches in his notebook and takes photos, ignoring admiring glances and smiles from ladies of all ages. Some even stop to chat; he's polite, but soon, getting the hint, they move on.

On our last morning in Paris, we visit the Conciergerie, an old castle that served as a prison during the Revolution. "So much bloodshed," Lou says, peering through the bars of a prison cell. "I don't know why you think the Revolution was so great, Sonia. It says here that some people even turned their own relatives in. Thousands died at the guillotine."

I wander to the display of Marie Antoinette's private cell. This is where the French queen waited for death, praying quietly, grieving the loss of home, husband, children. "The people did gain their freedom."

"But was it worth it?" He's standing in front of a painting of a girl serving a condemned man his last meal. "To lose so much for the sake of freedom. Shows you what a sick world this is."

"You sound like Sahara. She's always talking about how sinful everybody is. What about all the progress we've made? I mean, look at the two of us. Before the Revolution, could an Indian girl walk around Paris with a black boy from Louisiana? The world's a better place, Lou."

He takes a long second or two to look into my eyes, holding them like clay holds water. "If it is a better place, why do you look so sad?"

I guess he doesn't know about Baba—he's too new at school. I don't want to tell him. But how can I keep the door locked with those kind eyes searching mine? My throat gets tight, and I swallow, hard. "We'd better hurry," I say. "We're supposed to meet the rest of the group at the Sorbonne."

Storm clouds gather as we explore Paris's famous university, and a sudden downpour catches our group by surprise. Despite her amazing efficiency, Dr. Margot hasn't brought along seven umbrellas. She opens an enormous one over herself while the rest of us dash around, looking for shelter.

"Let's head in there," Lou says to me, pointing to the cathedral of Saint-Étienne-du-Mont.

"Meet you in an hour!" I call to the others, who are scampering into a café. Dr. Margot waves her permission and saunters after the others, staying dry under her massive umbrella.

Lou and I race to the cathedral. For once, hordes of other tourists aren't inside and the church is quiet. High marble arches circle the inside of the sanctuary, and a carved, filigreed screen divides it. Above the screen hangs a wooden figure on a cross.

Lou walks off. He stops in the center aisle, faces the front, and makes the sign of the cross. Then he slides into a pew and kneels to pray.

I'm surprised by the rush of affection I feel for him. And by the friendship that has been sculpted for us during these last few days. But if I'm honest, it's more than affection—this is how I used to feel about my literary crushes. I never thought I'd feel like that for someone in real life. And the best part is that I think he might feel the same way. At least, I *hope* he does. Somehow Paris has transformed Black Lightning and me into that oxymoron Sahara and I were talking about—a combination of contradictions that take on a new meaning together.

I walk down the center aisle, past where Lou is kneeling. Despite the rain, the stained glass gathers enough light to fill the cathedral with color. The windows glow in patterns of mustard, saffron, indigo, coral. Arches and vaults curve, soaring so high I can hardly see where they intersect. Statues of Mary, Jesus's mother, are tucked into corners with candles flickering at her feet. *Another strong woman*, I think. Bells begin to toll and then echo in the rafters. The glossy wood of the cross shines as if it's sweating. My eyes rest on the twisted, half-naked figure. So this is what happened to the man who liberated the adulterous woman. He, too, was attacked and condemned. And killed.

Talk about an oxymoron, I think. *The ultimate contradiction. A suffering God.*

Sahara told me once at an ERC meeting about how the women who loved him saw him dead and then alive again. *What would that have been like? To grieve, to ache, to be torn apart, and then . . . to hear his voice call your name again, feel the touch of his hand once more . . .*

"Baba," I whisper. "My Baba."

As if a strong wind has swept through the cathedral, the locked door inside me flies open. Six months' worth of tears begin to pour out, and I slide into a pew to weep. And weep some more.

Lou comes quietly to sit beside me. I sense him there, but my forehead is resting on the pew in front of me. I struggle to catch my breath, to look up, to explain. "My father—" I begin, but can't finish. I put my head down again. More tears. And more. Maybe they'll never stop.

Then, just as my sister had, just as my father always used to, Lou reaches over to take my hand in both of his. He holds it; he doesn't let go. I close my eyes, and the strong, gentle hands around mine become Starry's, and then Baba's, until finally I feel the scarred hands of an unseen Liberator sheltering my own.

Tara

Land Where My Fathers Died

B ABA'S ASHES MAKE IT TO BANGLADESH WITH-
out any hassle. Amit picks me up at Dhaka International Airport, looking sharp in a banker's suit and
tie. He gives me one of those upper-body-only, twist-to-the-
side half hugs that are perfectly appropriate between male
and female friends in America. Here, it earns me a nonverbal
scolding from Masjid, Amit's driver. *That's right,* I remember.
In Bengal, men and women don't touch in public. Bengalis
like Masjid learn early how to save ten minutes' worth of words
by raising an eyebrow, wrinkling a nose, or tipping a head at
a specific angle. Even kids are masters at the nonverbals.

The car whisks us to Amit's penthouse in the center of the city. The electricity is out for power rationing when we arrive, but thankfully, there's plenty of water. Masjid, who is Amit's driver *and* bearer (which, Amit informs me, is what male valets are called in Bangladesh), shows me into a guest room. I unpack and shower in candlelight. As the water pours over me, I fight back worries about being here. Amit's face lit up at the sight of me. Should I have come? Will he get the wrong idea *again*?

Sometimes I wish we'd met in a bar or a café. But no, we had to meet the old-fashioned Bengali way. Ma called to announce that Auntie Harm had found the perfect boy for me. We were scheduled to meet for lunch the following Saturday, she told me, just Amit and me. Thanks to a new lilt in Ma's voice, I couldn't bring myself to say no.

"They're trying to ARRANGE your marriage?" Sunny sputtered when she heard. "Are you CRAZY?"

It's just lunch, I said. *I'll never see him again.* But I did— he took me to a Knicks game and then the movies. We had dinner and went dancing. That's when he tried to kiss me good night for the first time, and I angled my head to offer a cheek. Even that didn't discourage him. More dinners, a concert, another Knicks game, his face in the front row of my shows, hands clapping hard.

And then he proposed. I could feel Ma and his parents and Auntie Harm waiting for good news as he held both of my hands. I couldn't look at his face when I said no.

Auntie Harm told me I was an idiot. Ma cried. Amit ignored his parents' advice and stayed my friend. A few months later, this time without any of our elders involved, he proposed again. My second, more private refusal must have sunk in, because that's when he accepted the assignment in Bangladesh. But that didn't keep him from sending me an aerogramme every week, which always ended the same way: *Come and visit. I'll help you keep your promise.* The last aerogramme added a postscript: *Only a few weeks left before I head back to New York. If you're going to come, Tara, you'd better come now.*

Masjid is nowhere in sight when I finally emerge in clean pajamas and a cotton robe. Thank goodness. No more shriveling looks of disapproval, at least not tonight. Amit is waiting on the screened verandah with cups of steaming mint tea. He's changed into a kurta and loose cotton pants. Candles in clay pots throw circles of flickering light across the clean tiles.

"Sorry there's load-shedding the first night you arrive, Tara. The power should be back soon, though. And the air-conditioning."

The two of us speak English to each other, even though we both grew up in homes where our parents spoke Bangla. We can both understand it, but his spoken Bangla is more fluent than mine. Growing up, he used it to talk to his parents; Sunny and I stuck to English at home even though our parents spoke Bangla.

"No problem," I say. "It's lovely out here." A song drifts up from an apartment below. I recognize it—"Utal Dhara Badal Jhare." Crap. The song my mother sang for my father the first time they met.

"At least you can't see Dhaka's urban sprawl," he says. "It's as dark and quiet tonight as in a village."

Warm winds carry the sweet smell of jasmine and the promise of rain. *This musical verandah scene is straight out of a cheesy Bollywood film*, I think. Time to break the mood. "What a whirlwind trip," I say brightly. "I can't believe they only gave me six days off—that's only four days here, counting travel! I should probably stay up all night so I'm still on New York time."

"A lot can happen in four days," he says.

"Mmmm," I say, sipping my tea and avoiding his eyes.

"Need a shoulder rub?" Amit asks, coming to stand behind me. The smell of jasmine now mingles with his aftershave.

"Definitely, after that flight."

I tilt my head forward. I can feel the soreness in my shoulders and neck even after a long shower. Amit's fingers probe, find the tightness, begin to battle it. I'm quiet, letting his strong fingers work on the knots of muscle.

Oh, how I've missed him! After he left, I was stunned by the Amit-shaped hole in my life. I like him. Heck, I might even grow to love him, but the thought of marrying a Bengali man? That feels like getting cast in a role without auditioning for it. No, thanks. I already look like Ma and sound like her. Do I have to *become* her, too? Every time Sunny looks in the mirror, she's reminded of Baba. But me? All I have left of our father is my driver's license, my U.S. passport, and my acting career. And I'm never giving any of those up, no matter how much Ma complains.

"Your shoulders feel like rocks," Amit says. "What's been going on?"

"Sunny and Ma fighting all the time."

"Over Lou?"

I nod.

"That's crazy. He's wonderful. I hate that part of our heritage so much."

"Me, too," I say, sighing. "Baba wasn't like that. Ma keeps begging Sunny to stop seeing him. And Sunny starts lecturing Ma about civil rights and racism the moment she comes home from college."

"I'm glad you moved back to the city. It was tough to concentrate on your career with all that squabbling in Ridgeford."

"I love my little apartment. Crazy how much Flushing felt like home when I moved back."

"Home? That reminds me—I have a surprise for you."

My stomach jumps. "I don't like surprises, Amit, remember?"

"You might like this one. At least, I hope so. I've booked the car for the whole day. After you're done in the river, Masjid is going to drive us to Poshora."

"Poshora?" We can both pronounce the *shaw* sound that's difficult for Americans. "Pasera," they might say instead, because their palates and ears don't form around Bangla. "You don't have to take me there—that wasn't part of my promise."

"I cleared extra hours for the jeep and driver. If you want, you can see Poshora."

I think for a moment. "I do want. This may be the only time I'll visit Bangladesh. But I can already imagine Takurdada's reaction if he were alive. His granddaughter visiting the 'shoythan Muslim family who stole our land.' Isn't it interesting how the Bangla word for 'evil' sounds like *Satan*?"

Amit settles the pillows behind me and sits down again, keeping a perfect "just friends" distance between us. "Hard to lose a big jute farm that's been in the family for generations. And to get nothing for it! Happened to my family, too, but at least they sold it for something."

"Sunny thinks Takurdada deserved it: *'He exploited his Muslim workers!'* And Baba agreed—*'God had a better plan for our family,'* he'd say. The man who took the house was Takurdada's foreman. I think his son still lives there."

"We do need to be careful, Tara. Families are trying to reclaim land lost at Partition. And Muslims are angry because the courts sometimes side with Hindus."

"Too late for our family," I say. "Takurdada tried, though. He must have sent fifty letters full of legal threats from Calcutta."

"When did he finally give up?"

"He didn't. Ignored his children, chewed betel leaves, and died a bitter old man."

"I guess your father never tried to get the property back."

"No, but I think he was sad about never seeing it again. He talked about Poshora like it was some kind of lost paradise."

"I'll take pictures for your grandchildren," Amit says.

He drops his pronouns casually but I feel the air tingle with the second one. *Your* grandchildren, he says, but is he thinking *our* grandchildren? I hope he isn't going to propose again. Because if he asks a third time, I might cave and say yes. Then Amit and I would become a Bengali couple in an arranged marriage, playing the same roles as our parents and grandparents and Das and Sen family ancestors have for generations. A twist of panic makes me stand and walk to the railing of the verandah. *Settle down, Tara*, I tell myself. *He's talking like a friend.* Maybe he's found a girl here to return his love. It's been ten months, right? And he's such a catch.

"How's the social life around here, Amit?" I ask. "You didn't write much about your friends."

"They're good people. Mostly expats. We play a lot of tennis at the American club. Ball boys for free—can you believe it? A foreigner never has to pick up a ball. The Australian club has the best parties, though. I'm taking you to one before you leave."

"Sounds good. I hope I survive tomorrow, though." If he wants to introduce me to his new friends, there's probably not a girlfriend around. Or maybe he's told her that his old buddy Tara is visiting?

He comes up behind me and fingers the collar of my robe. "I also have a present for you, Tara. It might help with the . . . the promise you made, and the visit to the village. Mrs. Masjid will bring it to you in the morning."

His arms are curving around my waist, and he's resting his chin on my shoulder. If there *is* a girlfriend around, she won't like this one bit. I resist for a minute, but then let myself lean back and close my eyes, relishing the feel of his strong body behind mine.

A dry cough sounds in the doorway, and Amit backs away immediately. It's Masjid. "Excuse me, sir. Would you kindly oblige by indicating whether Bearer should calendar your navy trousers for the morning?"

"No, thank you," Amit replies. "I'll wear the brown ones."

"As you wish, sir. I shall take my leave." Bowing stiffly, he throws me a glance and disappears.

Once again, his eyes fling disapproval over me like a heavy veil.

A gust of wind blows out the candle, and the monsoon rain begins to fall. Before I can react, Amit gently turns me around and gathers me close.

"I'm glad you're here, Star," he whispers under the percussion of the rain.

Baba's name for me. I wish he wouldn't use it. I pull out of his arms, glad I can't see his eyes in the darkness. "See you tomorrow. Good night, Amit."

I wake up early, jet-lagged, and watch the sun rise over Dhaka from my bed. Today, Amit and I are heading to the Padma River, a tributary of the Ganges, to deposit Baba's ashes. Simple and quick, that's my plan. I'm glad I don't have to do it in Calcutta, where relatives might insist on hiring a priest and inviting a crowd to watch one of my male cousins empty the urn and immerse himself in the river. Bangladesh—not India—is where Baba was born, on that jute farm the Das family lost during the war.

I made Ma promise not to tell our relatives I was coming to the country right across the border. I was a little surprised by how quickly she agreed, and that she didn't issue any directions about the urn. *I'm glad you're going*, was all she said. Sunny wanted to come along, of course, but she has final exams. And we can't both desert Ma.

There's a knock at my door. It must be Mrs. Masjid. A chubby lady, with a face as jolly as her husband's is dour, is giggling in the hall. She stands there holding a hanger and a valet's tray. "Good morning, good morning," she says. "These are from Mr. Amit. Shall I help you get dressed?"

My stomach jumps as I take stock of Amit's gift: a green silk sari, a blouse, a petticoat, golden bangles and dangly earrings, high-heeled sandals. I'm grateful for the skills that push my cheeks and mouth into a smile. "Let me brush my teeth first?"

"Of course, of course. Meantime, I will be preparing for Mr. Amit's lovely friend a nice cup of tea. Drink it, and then Mrs. Masjid can turn you into a real Bengali woman."

I spread Amit's gifts across the bed and sit on the edge of the mattress with my head in my hands. I've never worn a sari. The last time I even wore a salwar was at Baba's shradh ceremony. Since then, I've gained twenty pounds or so—I'm not ashamed, but I no longer have a mannequin's body. I don't need one. Unless I'm in a show, I never put on a costume. I nanny and go to auditions wearing simple black and white skirts and blouses, wear flat shoes, and rarely put on makeup or jewelry. "Ma still wearing her widow's uniform is one thing," Sunny complains, "but why are you dressing like a nun?"

I sigh and stroke the green fabric of the sari on the bed. I can tell by the soft, light silk and gold-threaded embroidery that it's an expensive one. Baba paid for the stylish

Western clothes I wanted, store-bought or Ma-made, but his eyes always lit up at the sight of Ma in a sari. I imagine that he would have loved to see me in one, though he'd never mentioned it. Today, of all days, maybe it's right that I put on a sari.

For you, Baba, I say, and open the door to Mrs. Masjid and her cup of tea.

The ferry pushes steadily through the currents of the Padma. Mid-morning sunshine spangles the water. Fishermen call greetings from rafts to sailing boats, and huge, silvery river dolphins leap unexpectedly into the air. Passengers perch on the open edges of the ferry, sipping tea from tiny china cups. They watch as Amit and I squeeze through lines of parked vehicles toward the tea-seller's stall.

Masjid stays with the car, guarding the urn. I wonder for a minute what he thinks about this journey of mine, especially since Islam forbids cremation.

I lean against a barrel and clutch my cup, aware of the curious eyes around us. I've mastered the nonverbals, so I can move and walk and talk like I grew up here. And now I'm wearing the costume—the breeze is making the perfectly pleated and tucked green silk cling to my body. It's easy for me to move in it; I've watched Ma model saris gracefully for years. I'm even traveling with a man who looks like he's the male lead in a Bollywood film. The American parts of me are nowhere in sight, so why are they staring?

Amit answers my unspoken question. "It's because you're so beautiful, Tara. I thought that color would look great on you. You look so much like your mother, it's scary."

I wince inside but force my face to light up with gratitude. "Everything fit perfectly, Amit. I'm not sure how you did that. Thanks for the bracelets and earrings, too. And the shoes." I lift one foot to show him the strappy, jeweled sandals that make me almost as tall as he is.

"I wasn't sure you'd want to go traditional, but I thought I'd give you the choice." He sips his tea and turns to watch the scenery. "Sorry about last night, by the way. Temporary insanity. I blame the load-shedding. The power must have turned off in my head, too."

I take a big gulp of hot tea myself, scald my mouth, and swallow hard. "It's okay, Amit. But maybe I shouldn't have come. I don't want to hurt you."

He nudges me, and points to a low country boat passing the ferry. "You missed me," he says. "That's why you came."

Inside the boat, five sand-haulers are fast asleep. They're so near each other they look like one big tangle of brown limbs and plaid lungee cloth. We watch until they disappear into the gray haze on the horizon.

"And, of course, to keep your promise," Amit adds. "Ready, Star?"

"Ready."

The ferry docks and Masjid drives along the river until we find a secluded area near the bank.

"Pop the boot, please," Amit tells Masjid. "And stay here."

Lifting the aluminum urn out of the trunk, Amit leads me down the bank to the rickety wooden platform.

"Want me to wait in the car?" he asks, handing me the urn.

I shrug. "Whatever you want. This won't take long. No son, so no immersion, no priest, no prayers."

I rest the urn on my hip and take off the lid. Standing at the edge of the water, I turn it upside down and give it a shake. The ashes scatter into the sunlit air, land on the surface, and sink almost immediately. A small lock of hair falls out of the urn after most of the ashes are gone. It floats instead of sinking and begins to drift away in the current.

I'd forgotten about the hair that Uncle Harm clipped before Baba's cremation. Part of me wants to leap into the river, grab the lock, and press it to my heart and lips before sending it off.

There, it's done. I've honored Baba as best I can. I wish

the Ganges could wash the grief from my heart, but it can't. Nothing can. I twist the lid back on the almost-empty urn. A few ashes still cling to the sides. They may have to stay there forever. I turn to face Amit, who's waiting on the bank. "What am I supposed to do with this thing now?"

"Give it to the poor?"

"Dirty, like this? Maybe. Baba would have liked that."

Amit reaches for my hand to help me up. "You okay?" he asks. "That was quick."

I shrug. "It had to be done. Wasn't easy, though."

He gives my hand a squeeze. "I'm glad I'm here with you. Next stop, Poshora."

We start driving again, and I watch the river twisting through the passing countryside. Spiky clumps of vegetation poke out of muddy rice paddies, fed by slim chains of water. If I'd grown up here, I'd know their names in Bangla. Hibiscus bushes lean over floating purple flowers like dancers trying to glimpse their own reflections.

Masjid turns on the radio, and Rabindra Sangeet adds the perfect soundtrack to the scene: "Por ke korile nikot bondhu"—*you bring the distant near.* One of Baba's favorites. I picture the lock of hair dancing in the current until it reaches the Bay of Bengal. When I asked to quit harmonium and Rabindra Sangeet lessons, Baba's face was sad, but he didn't argue. *For you, Baba*, I think again and begin to sing the words he loved.

It's the first time I've sung offstage in years. Masjid throws me a glance of surprise in the rearview mirror, and I catch a faint glimmer of a smile that he quickly extinguishes. That's one thing Bengali Muslims and Hindus share in common: the music of Rabindranath Tagore. "Door ke korile bhai"— *you make the stranger a brother*—I sing to the back of Masjid's head.

"I didn't know you were trained, Tara," Amit says.

"I took lessons for years," I answer. "Baba loved to hear me sing."

"I can see why. Reminds me of my mother. She's always singing Tagore around the house."

Another inward wince.

Another fake smile.

I stop singing.

We drive through the city of Faridpur and decide to pick up lunch at a market. Perfect. I can get some gifts for my return to Poshora. I wander through the stalls, enjoying the easy give and take of bargaining in Bangla. Ma taught me well. I don't get "insider" prices but my skills are good enough to earn respect from the sellers. And from Masjid. Meanwhile, he and Amit are using shoulders, elbows, legs, and chests to clear a path through the curious crowd pressing around us.

A blue sari embroidered with delicate gold flowers catches my eye, and I buy it, along with sweets, trinkets, and toys. When I'm done shopping, Amit buys a turmeric-stained cardboard container of lentils, egg, and rice, and we head back to the car to share it.

"I heard one man say he was sure you're a 'fillum' actress from India," Amit says, reaching into the container with his spoon.

"Maybe I should audition for a Bollywood movie. I might get a bigger part in Bombay than on Broadway."

Amit pops another big bite into his mouth. "Yum. This is good stuff. Another guy was convinced you were an oil magnate's wife from Dubai."

"Married to an Arab billionaire," I say. "Doesn't sound like too hard of a gig."

"Oh, definitely. He thought I was your bodyguard. He's not totally wrong. I'm all sweaty from pushing people away from you." He dabs his forehead with the towel that was his only purchase.

Masjid comes back chewing betel leaves, and we start driving again. As the jeep hurtles along, I tuck hundred-taka notes, worth about three dollars each, into folds of paper.

Masjid takes a wrong turn and stops for directions. The three of us climb out of the jeep into the heavy, still air of mid-afternoon. Purple and blue cotton saris are slung across the open windows of a clay house. A breeze lifts the light material, and I glimpse three babies sleeping side by side on a bamboo cot.

An elderly man stands by the door, smiling toothlessly. He's wearing a white dhoti instead of a lungee, which marks him as one of the few remaining Hindus in Poshora. "Das Family House?" he repeats after Masjid. "Yes, yes. Still standing. Last house down that lane, about three kilometers, just past the bridge."

"Thank you, Uncle," Amit says.

The old man peers up at me through thick lenses. "So you've come back, have you? High time. That son of a scoundrel will be troubled to see the face of a Das again."

I nod, too surprised to answer. I've been told for years that I don't look anything like Baba. How did he spot the Das in my face?

The jeep turns onto a narrow, muddy road. We rattle over a bridge into a clearing, and Masjid turns off the engine. "Das Family House," he announces, like a conductor at the end of the line.

I scan the property. A square bungalow, paint peeling,

faded green shutters closed against the afternoon sunshine. Two huge mango trees laden with fruit, shading a bench on a wide, grassy space in front of the house. A winding path, lined with purple and white bougainvillea, and water sparkling in the distance. Tops of countless fruit trees in a grove behind the house. Beyond, jute fields stretch out to the horizon, with no other house in sight. It looks just as Baba had described it.

I climb out of the jeep. "I'm going to knock."

"I'm coming with you," Amit says.

Before we reach the door, a man wearing a lungee opens it. He comes out of the house and shuts the door firmly behind him, but I glimpse a row of eyes peering through the slats of the window shutters.

"What do you want?" the man demands, his eyes shifting from us to the World Bank insignia on the jeep. "You have no business here."

Amit touches his hand to his forehead. "Salaam. We don't want to trouble you."

"What *do* you want, then?"

I hold out the bag of presents. "I brought gifts for your children before departing for my home in America. I am the daughter of Rajeev Das." My father's name rings loudly from my mouth. It's the first time I've heard it spoken since Ma identified his body in the hospital. It feels like I'm inviting Baba to join us here. *For you, Baba. This is for you.*

The man's eyes are focused on me, measuring the unspoken language that will either threaten him or put him at ease. I avert my gaze and still my body.

Suddenly, the man claps his hands twice. "Bring tea!" he shouts. Muffled responses come from inside the house. Pots and pans clatter and a baby starts to wail.

The man leads us to the shady bench. "You will stay with me," he says to Amit. "Your wife can wander as she pleases. After tea."

Neither of us correct his take on our relationship. As he begins to lecture Amit about the state of the Bangladeshi economy, I sit quietly and finish my fourth cup of tea since the morning. Inside the house, I hear laughter and conversation, the sounds of women enjoying each other's company.

"May I go inside?" I ask.

The man sweeps his palm toward the door. "Please. I have many things to tell your husband about the banking system here."

Amit rolls his eyes and winks at me, making sure the man doesn't see him. I pick up the bag of presents and make my way to the house where my father was born. Again, the door flies open before I can knock. A tide of women and girls surrounds me on the threshold and pulls me inside. Curious hands smooth the material of my sari, finger my bracelets, caress the skin of my forearms. A flood of questions in village Bangla swirls around me; I can hardly understand the dialect.

The front room doesn't contain much furniture. A few old jute chairs are scattered here and there and a faded jute rug covers the floor. No pictures on the walls, and the paint is peeling. I wonder for a second if anything I see was left behind by my family thirty or so years ago. It certainly all looks ancient. Maybe the baby version of Baba crawled across that rug.

A young girl pulls the least rickety chair under a fan and wipes it clean with a cloth. Two of the oldest women seat me, like handmaidens attending a queen. I count thirty-five female faces in the smiling circle around me. Shy children peer out from behind their saris.

"Come," I say, reaching into my bag. I spread out the toys and sweets, and the children scurry forward, eyes bright. I tuck envelopes into their shirts while their mothers try to stop me.

"You should not give this kindness to us," one of them protests.

"It's my privilege," I answer. "Where is your newest bride?"

The girl who dusted the chair is pushed forward. "She has married our third son," the oldest woman says.

I hand the girl the blue-and-gold sari. She takes it, lightly traces one loop of the embroidery, grins at me, and slips away. A toddler tries to climb onto my lap, his naked body camouflaged in talcum powder. He tugs at my sari, frowning, demanding. In English, softly, I tell him: "It's yours. Yours to *keep*. We don't want it back."

He's whisked away to make room for biscuits and more tea. My fifth cup. The questions come faster now. "Is your husband a good man?"

I decide to respond with the head waggle that means yes. I'm not lying; Amit *is* a good man. Besides, it's better if they assume he's my husband. In this village, I'd have been married off at eighteen at the latest, and we probably would have two or three children by now.

And that, of course, is their next question. "Children?"

This time I have to use words. "I don't have any."

The oldest woman reaches for my hand. "We will pray to Allah. What is your name?"

"Tara. Tara Das."

"Tara! It's a perfect name for you—'star'! Be blessed, my daughter."

Suddenly, I can't speak. Those words. That name. In this

house, it's right. Tears slide down my cheeks, and the women dab their own eyes, even though they don't know why we're crying. Again and again, the matriarch of the household wipes my sadness away with the end of her sari.

When I stand to go, a chorus of protests arises. Old and young women, their hands caressing, cluster around me as I make my way to the door. I turn for one last look, one last smile, before stepping into the empty courtyard. The door closes behind me.

Amit is still on the bench, pretending to listen to the man's one-sided lecture. He tries to catch my eye, but I ignore his "get over here, please" look. Instead, I go back to the jeep, ask Masjid to open the trunk, and take out the almost-empty urn.

I wander down the path into the garden and through the fruit trees, recognizing landmarks from stories Baba told. A clay building houses chickens in cool, connected holes. Here my father ran his hand along the length of a sleeping python as he hunted for morning eggs. The path curves through the trees toward the pond, and I squint into the sunshine sparkling across the water, knowing that in places it's too deep to measure. Here a great-uncle drowned when he was three. I count the trees: thirty-two banana trees, seven guava trees, fourteen mango trees, countless coconut and lychee trees.

Here, in the great storm of 1936, lightning destroyed the tallest mango tree in Poshora. Resting the urn on the stump of the dead tree, I can almost hear Baba's voice guiding me.

There's a stone ghat for washing clothes at the edge of the pond. Standing on it, I lean over and dip the urn in the water. I fill and empty it, again and again, until all traces of ash and hair are gone. It's clean now. And then I catch sight of my reflection. The watery face does look like my mother's, but I remember the old man who gave us directions. I look closer at the water. I, too, can see the Das family imprint there now. I'm Baba's girl, too, and nothing will change that.

I splash my face with water, then dry it on my scarf. Carrying the clean urn, I head back to the bench. Behind me, black crows rise from the trees, flying west against a fading sky, calling to one another.

Amit stands to meet me. "Ready to go, Tara?" he asks. He sounds eager.

I turn to the landowner. "Have you found any old letters or papers that belonged to my family?"

The man frowns. "We kept a trunk of some such things. Photographs, letters, school certificates. But nobody came for them."

"May I have them?"

He hesitates. "My father took care of them."

I step forward to catch and hold his eyes. "What did he do with them?"

The answer comes in a low voice: "He burned them."

There's a silence.

"I am sorry for that," he says finally.

I hand him the urn. "Can you put this to good use? Our family is finished with it."

He knows what it is but accepts it anyway. "I'll use it to water the trees," he promises.

"Salaam," I say, meaning goodbye. And then, in full view of all watching eyes, flagrantly disregarding ancient rules about women and men touching in public, I take Amit's hand and walk away.

I point out landmarks as we head to the mango grove, and he takes a few pictures. Standing beside the dead stump, I look up and see a golden piece of fruit dangling from an overhanging branch. It glimmers in the last light like an oversize jewel. It's out of reach, so I hoist myself up on the stump, sari and all, resting one hand on Amit's shoulder for balance.

"Get it?" he asks, steadying my ankles with his strong grip.

"Got it," I say, hopping back down.

Peeling the skin back with my teeth, I bite into the flesh, knowing that in Amit's presence, I can eat it Bengali-style.

"Tasty?" he asks.

I offer it to him, and he takes a bite. "Sweet, like the giver," he says.

Baba's voice inside my head gives me courage: *Be blessed, my Star.*

I answer him with the truth: *For me, Baba. For me.*

"Ripe and ready," I tell Amit, and look into his face, letting him see the desire and acceptance and hope in my eyes.

"Really? Wait. Wait. What? Tara, what are you saying?"

I move closer. He studies my expression again, and slowly, slowly tips my chin up. Our first kiss is much sweeter than the mango's juice. I'm dizzy with the desire that sweeps through me from sandal to necklace. Amit pulls away first. Holding me steady, he hurls the half-eaten fruit as far as he can. It lands with a distant, muted splash in the pond. And then, in the land where my fathers died, he takes me in his arms and kisses me again.

No Translation

RANEE FROWNS AT HER GARDEN THROUGH THE sliding glass door. Weeds have overcome her husband's herbs, but she still tends to the tomatoes—his favorite—that glow on the vine every summer. Strange how that word has no Bangla translation. *TO-mah-to*, they'd called them in her village, with the accent on the first syllable, making no distinction between singular and plural.

It's time to harvest them again. Already. She got so tired last year. And for what? The bags she filled grew soggy with juice, the tomatoes soft and squashy. She threw them away.

He'd taken such delight in his tomatoes and peppers, planting a raised vegetable bed after they moved into the house. "Now we're Americans," he said, and threw his arms around her in the privacy of their room. The "Master Suite," he liked to call it, even though the girls teased him.

She wanders through the empty rooms that they took such delight in decorating. The living room, where he'd placed a big, lighted showcase to display the vases she'd started collecting. Porcelain, copper, ceramic, bronze. They line the shelves, quiet, waiting, like her. The dining room, where the three of them relished her cooking and chatted so easily about their days, as though they had an endless supply ahead.

Moving to this quiet New Jersey neighborhood—owning a bit of land after his family lost the ancestral property during the war—restored him. This house and garden brought back the sweet man she had begun to love after their wedding, before the pregnancies, the miscarriages, the moves, and the money worries.

Or maybe the sweetness started in their Flushing apartment, after their daughter's written words had exposed her contempt and erased the sharpness from her tongue. Toward him, at least. She made him happy after that. Or at least tried to.

For two short years. That's all they were given in this home.

She tries not to think about it, but his . . . the accident

hit the girls hard. No wonder Sonia chose to run into the arms of that boy. If only she hadn't gone to Paris! But winning that essay contest was the first thing to make her smile since the accident. She and that boy came back and soon said they were "in love"—whatever that means before you get married.

Then they went off to the same college.

Ranee prayed to her gods, hoping that their gifted daughter, the sweet "Mishti" of her father's heart, would find someone else. Anyone but this boy. But it didn't happen.

Sonia graduated and got a job with the *New York Times*. Brilliant girl. So proud, her Baba would have been. And the boy? He decided to become a full-time sculptor, his black hands stained from the pots he shapes and tries to sell.

And then, no matter how much Ranee objected, how many tears she cried, how she begged and invoked her husband's memory, the disaster came.

Sonia eloped.

Ranee hasn't spoken to her youngest daughter since Tara came with the news. *Sunny's married and living in Harlem, Ma. With Lou's family.*

Mrs. Johnson, the boy's mother, is a loud, big woman; Ranee saw her once by chance in a grocery store before they moved out of Ridgeford. They didn't speak, but they each knew who the other one was—the mother of the child my child chose without my permission.

This is what America gives us? Ranee thinks in disgust. Why did she push her husband to come here? Maybe they should have returned to Calcutta after London. But even now she recoils at the thought of living with her own in-laws.

No, Ranee can never go back to India. All that waits for her there is shame. She'll die here in New Jersey. Or maybe New York. Tara and Amit have been asking her to move to Flushing, to be near them, and maybe she will. It's lonely here.

The last photo taken of the Das family sits on the kitchen counter. Sonia is tucked under her father's strong arm, and Tara is squeezed between her parents. Ranee gazes at the three faces that used to gather around her table every evening and fingers the pleats of her white widow's sari.

Sonia used to try to convince her to wear colorful clothes, but it didn't work. Every morning, Ranee folds and tucks a long, plain ivory or white cloth around herself, fingers recalling the complicated maneuvers she learned as a teenager. It's the least she can do for him.

The phone sits beside the photo. Suddenly, it chimes and blinks. Ranee rushes to answer it. "Tara? Is that you?"

"No. It's me, Ma. Sonia."

Ranee can't speak; her heart is hammering. *How long has it been? Two years? Almost three?*

"I have to see you, Ma."

Hope rises high in Ranee's throat, and she can't keep it out of her voice. "Did you leave him, darling?"

There's a pause on Sonia's end this time, and Ranee waits, crushing the hem of her sari into her fist.

"No, Ma. Lou's right here. But I'll come alone. May I visit this afternoon?"

She glances at the tomatoes bursting with juice. "Of course," she says, before she changes her mind. She puts down the phone, and wanders into the kitchen, feeling dizzy. Why is Sonia coming home? If she's not leaving him, does she think her mother will forgive her? Maybe she should; her husband would have wanted her to.

She decides to wait and see what her daughter has to say. It will take about an hour for Sonia to arrive. Ranee goes to the garden, empty paper bag in hand. Stooping and harvesting tomatoes, she tries to settle her nerves by escaping into the safety of memories, when her skin was smooth as milky tea, her hair black as a crow's wing. *She sends Tara to call them to dinner. Her husband is with Sonia, listening to their youngest recite poetry in that beautiful lilting voice of hers: "I wandered lonely as a cloud, that floats on high o'er vales and hills . . ."*

The doorbell rings. Ranee hurries inside carrying a full bag of tomatoes. Five feet from the door, she sees a silhouette through the frosted glass panel. It's shaped like the bulky water jug her mother-in-law gave her, the one Ranee always hated.

She opens the door, but her daughter stays outside. Ranee's eyes take in the familiar round face, dark skin, big eyes, short, strong neck. Sonia's shoulders are wide, like Ranee's husband's used to be. But further down, gender erases any resemblance between them.

Inside the curved container of their daughter's womb, a stranger is growing. Generations of ancestors hurl accusations inside Ranee's mind. "You were too permissive," they sneer. "It's your fault."

She can barely hear Sonia's voice. "Say something, Ma," Sonia is begging. "Please."

Ranee keeps her eyes on the ripeness of her daughter's belly and obeys the voices. "You dishonor your father's memory."

Sonia's voice dwindles to a whisper. "No, Ma. I don't. But you do. Baba would have welcomed all three of us."

She's right, and they both know it. Suddenly, Ranee is furious. At herself. She's too weak. She's failed them all. At him, even now, after all these years. How could he have left her alone to handle this impossible job?

"Your father's dead," she says, and closes the door.

Framed in the frosted glass panel, the squat outline waits, dwindles, and then disappears.

Ranee stares at the bag she's holding. Juice is starting to leak from it, staining the hall carpet, but she can't bring herself to throw it away.

3
Settlers
1998–2006

Chantal

New Rules

N O WAY," I SAY. "*BOTH* QUEENS HAVE TO be the same color."

"Says who?" Grandma Rose is sitting next to me on the sofa, turning cards over to find pairs. The player who finds the most pairs wins. She's trying to match a queen of hearts with a queen of clubs.

"You know the rules." I glance at my watch. One hour until my Kathak lesson.

"Stupid rules," Grandma says, but she puts the queens back on the coffee table. We've been playing this game together since I was five. And today Grandma Rose's turns take so long, it feels like this one match has gone on for ten straight years.

Spicy smells drift out from the kitchen. Didu, my other grandmother, is making chicken curry and biryani rice. She visits us here in Harlem once a month or so, spending a couple of nights on the sofa bed in Mom's office. The rest of the time, she lives in Aunt Tara and Uncle Amit's Manhattan penthouse, which is three times the size of our apartment. It's no surprise that it's so luxurious. Aunt Tara's a movie star, and Uncle Amit's a banker. The two of them and my cousin Anna live mostly in Mumbai, in their *other* luxury home. They visit New York every now and then, but the grandmother we share stays in their Manhattan penthouse all the time. That she visits us, the Johnson family, at all is a miracle, now that I know the whole story. It's become lore.

Mom and Didu didn't speak for years because Didu didn't want my parents to get married. Not even when I showed up. But after Anna was born thirteen years ago, Mom insisted on hosting her first rice-tasting ceremony—something the family never did for me—here in our Harlem apartment. Aunt Tara and Uncle Amit somehow convinced Didu to join the party. Dad says that as soon as I saw my grandmother, I toddled over, lifted my arms, and in the sweetest voice possible, said, "Dee-doo," which sounds exactly like the Bangla word for "grandmother." How I'd learned the word nobody knew, because this was the first time I'd laid eyes on her. I probably needed a diaper change, but to all the grown-ups it sounded like I was calling my maternal grandmother by name. The story concludes with high drama like a Bengali soap opera. Didu burst into tears, swept me into her arms, and cuddled me close. Everybody bawled, there was some kind of massive family reconciliation, and Didu hasn't let go of me since.

The only two adults in the Johnson family who don't get along now are my grandmothers. Even Grandpa and Didu are polite to each other. But Grandma Rose doesn't have much to say to Didu. You'd think she wouldn't show up during Didu's visits, but here I am on a hot afternoon, stuck playing cards again with the most intense Concentration player on the planet.

My grandmothers like to win at everything, including grandmothering. My Carver classmates complain about challenging classes and competitive sports, but they don't know the meaning of the word "stress." Try spending hot July afternoons with two competitive grandmothers. During the school year it isn't so bad, because Grandma Rose works full-time as Carver's drama teacher, so she doesn't come around as much. But during the summers, my grandmothers collide. Both of them adore me, don't get me wrong, but on a long, sticky day like today, adoration and suffocation can feel like first cousins.

"Kareena wants to see you, Chantal," Grandma tells me, sounding nonchalant as she looks over the cards. "In person."

Grandma's a good actress, but she can't fool me. I know what she wants. Every summer, she selects a rising senior to be in charge of the summer show—to pick the script, cast the players, and direct the whole thing. My friend Kareena's been Grandma Rose's right-hand apprentice since her freshman year, so when Grandma Rose picked her, it was no surprise.

Kareena decided to write this year's show herself. It stars a noble African queen who tries to defend her tribe from advancing slave traders. And yesterday, *only* to make Grandma Rose happy, I auditioned for the part of the queen. I'm no actress, but I can tell Kareena's script is amazing. She's one of the best writers at Carver, and her queen's last speech got me choked up—*and* fired up. Thanks to black pride on Dad's side of the family, it's easy to imagine a strong, passionate African woman as one of my ancestors.

"I just know she's going to give you that role," Grandma Rose says, matching a pair of twos.

"Grandma! Did you say anything to her?" If Kareena feels

pressured to cast me in the lead, it won't benefit her beautiful play.

"No, Chantal, I didn't," Grandma Rose says haughtily. "You know that for the student-run productions, I just show up for performances."

"Good. Because the principal gives you a lot of power at that school, Grandma Rose."

That gets her smiling again.

It's my turn now. I haven't been paying attention to the cards, so my first flip reveals the queen of hearts again. Where *is* that stupid queen of diamonds? Oh, great. Now I've found the idiotic queen of spades. I turn her back over.

Another one of Grandma's excruciating turns. She flips the black queen right back over and studies the remaining cards, trying to finish me once and for all by picking the queen of clubs.

I spot Mom in the hallway. She's a journalist who covers women's rights issues. Plus, now she's writing a book about girls who are married off when they're young—yes, that still happens—so she stays locked in her office, popping out every now and then for snacks. Today, her baggy T-shirt reads: BODIES: NOT FOR SALE. She heads toward the living room, where we are, but starts quietly backing away as soon as she spots Grandma Rose.

"Hey, Mom," I say loudly.

Mom gives me an "I know what you did there" look. "Hello, Rose. Hi, Shanti."

"Shanti," which means peace in Bangla, is what everybody in the family calls me, except for Grandma Rose. She insists on using "Chantal," the French name my Paris-loving parents made official at my baptism. I'm named after one of my mom's writer heroes, but I think Grandma Rose likes it because it's French, and not Indian. And because of her, I'm Chantal to everyone at school, too.

"Hello, Sonia," Grandma says to Mom, not looking up.

"Winning again, Rose?"

"Almost. Your mother's in the kitchen, making that chicken dish again."

"Great. Seen your dad, Shanti?" Mom asks.

"Bedroom," I answer, and Mom practically races back down the hall. My parents disappear a lot when the grandmothers are together.

Grandma Rose snorts. Nobody snorts like Grandma Rose. "Those two. Still carrying on like they're a match made in heaven," she says, unfurling the words one by one in her slow, French-tinged Louisiana accent.

No thanks to you and Didu, I think. But I don't say it aloud. Dad's parents accepted their relationship earlier than

Didu, but I've heard Dad describing Grandma Rose's first re-action to Mom: " 'Lou, darling, I know young men sometimes lose their heads over someone exotic. A lot of lovely American girls are waiting for a fine man like you.' " She said "American," but she meant black. It's 1998, and you still don't often see someone like my father and someone like my mother in the same family. Blacks and whites, maybe a few. But blacks and Bengalis? Never, in my experience. Which means there probably aren't many other people like me out there.

Grandma Rose finally finds the queen of clubs, matches all four queens, and ends this game. She's spreading out her large stack of winning pairs when Didu comes with a tray of tea cups, a tea kettle, and a plate of cookies.

"This should fill us up nicely until dinner," Didu says, setting her tray on top of the cards. She speaks English when she visits, unless she's talking only to Mom.

"Which we'll eat at midnight," whispers Grandma Rose in my ear. We do usually eat late when Didu cooks, but Mom says late dinners are common for Bengalis.

I hope Didu hasn't heard, but she sighs. Nobody sighs like Didu. "American chickens are very hard. They take a long time to cook." She plops down on the other side of me, squashing me into a grandmother sandwich.

Ever since that day when Didu fell in love with me, my

grandmothers act like toddlers who want the same toy. Over tea, they tell stories about summertime when *they* were teenagers. Grandma Rose talks about how she was the first fifteen-year-old in her Baton Rouge neighborhood to wear a two-piece bathing suit. Didu talks about winning first prize in a dance contest the summer *she* was fifteen, and how everyone raved over her feet with their henna designs.

I *think* that's what they're talking about, anyway. I can't tell for sure because they're talking at the same time, interrupting each other and throwing in my name every other sentence to grab my attention. I twist my head from side to side like I'm at a tennis match and steal another glance at my watch. Thirty long minutes until Kathak. *Wait, Kareena wants to see me, right? Maybe I'll use her as an excuse.* I take a big gulp of the sweet, milky, cardamom-flavored tea. Didu takes it personally when I don't finish something she prepared for me.

"I think I'll stop by Kareena's for a few minutes," I say, breaking into the "conversation" once my cup is empty.

Grandma Rose smiles. "You've got talent in your blood, Chantal. Can't wait to hear what happens."

"Speaking of talent in the family," Didu says. "Did you hear your Auntie Tara's new film opens next month, Shanti?"

I nod. I have heard. Many times. While Uncle Amit was first posted in Mumbai, Aunt Tara was "discovered" by a

Bollywood director. Now she's a star in India, I guess, and my cousin is being raised in Mumbai like a Bengali princess by *her* other set of grandparents. Didu, of course, brags about Anna all the time: speaks Bangla fluently, prefect at her school (which sounds too much like *perfect*), sews and embroiders her own clothes, was featured as a young animal-rights hero in the *Times of India*, wins debate competitions in Mumbai, blah, blah, blah.

Grandma Rose is sipping her tea slowly, and I can almost sense her counting to ten—advice she gives to argumentative Carver students. I've never seen it work when she tries it herself. This time, she gets to about seven. "Tara managed to land a small role or two in New York before they left, didn't she?" she asks. It's not really a question. It's Grandma scoring a point.

"Yes," Didu answers. "But her talent was wasted here, because she doesn't only act—she sings beautifully, too."

"She didn't want to try out for Broadway musicals, then?" Another question that isn't. Grandma Rose is a master at those.

Didu's no weakling. "Why settle for something less challenging? My daughter can sing any American song after listening to it two or three times, but have you ever seen an American who can master a Tagore song?"

Who would want to? I wish I couldn't read Grandma Rose's mind. I'm glad she doesn't say it out loud.

Didu's still evening the score. "Even our dancing requires more rhythm and grace and beauty. Which reminds me, we are needing to leave in fifteen minutes, Shanti."

"I'll meet you outside, Didu. I have to go change."

"Can you come back and let me know Kareena's news before your lesson?" Grandma Rose asks.

"No time," Didu says.

I look at Grandma Rose. I look at Didu. "I'll try, Grandma. But my teacher hates it when we're late."

I squeeze my way out through the grandmothers and head to my room. My cousin and I both started Kathak lessons when we were small. Anna took classes in Mumbai while I studied here in New York. But Anna quit early while I kept going. Turns out that Little Miss India's too petite for Kathak; the dance works better with a body like mine. It's the one Bengali thing I'm better at than my cousin. Muscular thighs; long, lean limbs and fingers; and a strong butt come in handy for all those twists, bends, and squats. I love the way that the bells on my ankles and wrists keep time to the mathematical rhythm of the tabla drum. And I'm good at the body vocabulary that tells a story without having to use any spoken language.

I put on my salwar, dangly earrings, and lipstick, and I'm almost ready. When I emerge, the grandmothers are still sitting silently on the sofa with a Shanti-size space between them.

Grandma Rose wrinkles her nose at my Indian outfit. "I have no idea how you dance in all that," she says, her hands fluttering up and down and side to side in arcs so wide I might be wearing a nun's habit.

"Come with us and find out, Grandma," I say. "I could use the moral support."

I'm actually hoping for a lead role in the upcoming Kathak recital. It's the first show choreographed by our new teacher, and she's assigning parts today. No speaking required, just dancing.

Didu stretches out a hand and I use my quad strength to heave her to her feet. "You are the best dancer in that class, Shanti," she tells me. "If only your hair were a bit longer."

I keep my hair short and natural. My Bengali mom wears her hair cropped close to her head, too. But Didu's expressed her opinion clearly: she prefers long hair.

"Your hair is perfect, Chantal," Grandma Rose says. "It shows off your long neck and strong shoulders—got both of those from your daddy, didn't you, honey?"

If looks could kill, Grandmother Rose's funeral would

be tomorrow. "I am going to freshen up," Didu says, picking up the tea tray. "I'll meet you outside, Shanti."

After she leaves, there's another snort from the sofa. "Freshen up? How? All she wears is that white sari, no makeup, no jewelry. The neighborhood's calling her 'Mother Teresa.'"

Grandma Rose reaches up *her* hand, and I haul *her* up off the couch. "Thanks, sweetie. Hurry and go see Kareena. Can't wait to hear what she says."

Probably that I suck at acting, I think, but I don't say it aloud. The sandals Aunt Tara sent me from India are waiting by the front door next to Didu's old-lady tennis shoes. Meanwhile, Grandma Rose's size-ten high-heeled pumps are still firmly on her feet. She refuses to take them off when she visits, even though it's an Indian custom to leave your shoes at the door. The rest of us do it automatically now, even Dad and Grandpa.

Kareena's building is two doors down, and she's outside on the front stoop with Jenna. A turban made of kente cloth, necklaces made of glass beads, and a rainbow of bandanas are spread out on the stairs. Jenna, who landed in our neighborhood from Somalia last year, is a Carver full-ride scholarship junior like me, also recruited by Grandma Rose. My grandmother is single-handedly peppering that mostly all-white school with dark faces.

"What's with the accessories?" I ask my friends.

Kareena looks up from the bandana she's tying around Jenna's waist. "Oh, hey, Chantal. You look great, as usual. We're trying to work out a sticky part in the play. I can't quite figure out the staging, and it helps my creative flow to see it acted out in costume."

"The script is so good, Kareena," I tell her, with another quick look at my watch. Ten minutes till Kathak. "It's going to be a huge hit. Grandma said you wanted to see me? Sorry I don't have much time; I'm heading to my dance class."

"Oh. Um, well, this is hard, Chantal, but I wanted to tell you that Jenna's going to be the queen. I hope Mrs. Johnson won't be upset."

I didn't want the part, so why does this sting? "She said it was up to you," I say slowly, thinking of the hope in Grandma Rose's eyes.

"Tell her Jenna's got talent. Plus, she was *born* in Africa. She's perfect—just look at her. Jenna, stand still."

Kareena ties the bandana and drapes Jenna in the beaded glass necklaces. I watch Jenna trying to fit the kente turban over her head scarf. We're all black girls; you can't hide that.

But if Jenna's darkness is midnight-lights-out-no-moon, and Kareena's a half crescent lighter, then mine would be what's left of the dark on a full-moon night. If my skin were darker, would I look more like the magnificent, powerful woman Kareena needs for her play?

Jenna studies my expression. "Maybe Chantal can be my understudy, Kareena?" she asks, her African accent swinging back and forth like a bell.

Hmmmm . . . It's highly unlikely that Jenna would get sick, so I wouldn't actually have to act. Maybe that would satisfy Grandma Rose? "Yes, what about that, Kareena? Or some minor no-speaking part?"

Kareena swings a hand palm-down in my face, smiling. "Oh, stop it, Chantal. You and I both know you only auditioned to make your grandmother happy. What I really need is for you to handle my production budget—use those mad math skills of yours to pay for ads and stuff like that."

I sigh, sounding weirdly like Didu, even to me. "Okay, okay, get me the numbers. I'll start crunching them."

"Thanks. Do you want to tell Mrs. Johnson, or should I?"

"I'll do it."

Didu comes out of our apartment building. "Good afternoon," she says to Kareena and Jenna without really looking at them. She's been visiting in this neighborhood for thirteen years and still doesn't know Kareena's name.

"Hello, Mrs. Das," says Kareena.

Jenna's still old-world enough to do better with the greeting: "Good afternoon, Grandmother Das," she says, bowing her head slightly.

The courtesy and accent lure Didu's eyes to Jenna's face, and then to her head scarf. "What is your name? Are you from Ghana?"

"Jenna. I'm from Somalia, Grandmother."

I can tell Didu likes the title. "Muslim?" she asks.

"Yes, Grandmother."

That answer doesn't please Didu as much. She turns to me. "Let's go, Shanti, we are going to be late," she says. "No time to head back home now."

"I'll get you the numbers tomorrow!" Kareena calls after me.

I try not to picture Grandma Rose's reaction when I tell her Kareena wants me to be a budgetary assistant. Let's just hope I get a decent role in the recital. At least that would make *one* of my grandmothers happy.

The Indian Dance Academy of New York uses a studio at the Y. As the other students arrive, Didu takes stock of them from head to toe while I tighten the bracelets of bells around my ankles. The teacher walks in, hauling a huge cassette player. She plugs it into an outlet beside us and presses "play." Tabla music fills the studio, and my spirits rise with the beat.

"Hello, Mrs. Das," Ms. Singh says. Her accent is 100 percent American, and she never addresses Didu as "Auntie" or greets us with a Namaste. My grandmother's come twice since Ms. Singh started teaching. And both times she's left the class muttering about Ms. Singh's lack of manners.

Eleven other advanced Kathak dancers line up to practice. The rest of them are fully Indian, but Uma is the only other Bengali in the class. She's a good dancer, too, but her braids keep whipping around and whacking me. I glance over at Didu, who's sitting in one of the chairs set up for parents and grandparents. Her old-lady shoes are keeping time with the tabla, and her eyes are focused only on my hands, face, and feet. Stepping away to widen the space between Uma and me, I concentrate on the rhythm of the music, the thump of feet, the jangle of silver, and the story the twelve of us are telling. Bends, turns, eye movements, hand gestures—I'm good at all of them. I forget the audience completely, something I can never do when I act.

When the music stops, Didu's the only onlooker who

bursts into applause. "Darun, Shanti! Tui ey-class-eh shobche bhalo nach-ish!" she calls to me in lilting Bangla.

I'm not exactly sure what she said, but Uma's mother scowls. I wipe my sweaty face with a towel and force myself to return my grandmother's proud smile.

"Gather around, dancers!" calls Ms. Singh. "You've all done so well. It was difficult to assign the parts for our recital. We have two lead roles in the dance—a princess and a prince."

I hold my breath.

"Uma will be the princess," Ms. Singh says.

Didu hauls herself to her feet and marches over to us. "UMA?! Have my ears gone bad?"

Uma's mother gasps.

"It's okay," I whisper when Didu reaches my side.

"No, Shanti. You are the best dancer in this class." Her voice is bold and firm.

She's right, I think suddenly. My body bends and twirls with more strength and grace than the others; my eyes and hands are better storytellers. But I don't speak up. My cheeks feel even hotter than they did while I was dancing.

Didu turns to face Ms. Singh. "My granddaughter should play the princess."

"I'm sorry, Mrs. Das," Ms. Singh answers. "I've already made my decision."

My grandmother's feet are apart, both fists are on her hips, and her stance makes her look like a burly wrestler in spite of the white sari. Or maybe because of it. "But why? Isn't Shanti's technique far superior? Surely you can see that?"

Ms. Singh shakes her head. "Your granddaughter's talented, I'm not denying that. But for my recitals, I have to think about how the dancers *look* as well as how they dance. Shanti's—well, her appearance is just right for the role of the prince. It's a big part, also, don't worry. Okay, let's move on. The rest of you will be their subjects . . ."

Didu and I walk home together. Judging by the Bengali mumbling beside me, she's still fuming. *Great.* I'm batting a thousand when it comes to grandmother disappointment.

Grandma Rose is napping on the sofa when we walk through the door. She sits up, takes one look at my face, and pats the space beside her. "What's wrong, Chantal?"

I leave my sandals by the door and collapse on the sofa. "I didn't get the role I wanted in the Kathak recital."

Grandma Rose puts her arm around me. "What?! I thought you were the best dancer in that class."

"That she is," Didu says, slowly taking off her shoes.

"I'm playing the *prince*," I tell Grandma Rose. "Apparently Uma looks more like a princess than I do."

"What's wrong with that teacher? Is she blind?"

"As a rat," Didu says.

As a bat, I think, but I don't correct her English. Didu hates that. Instead, I lean my head on Grandma Rose's shoulder. May as well tell all the bad news at once. Guess I won't be a princess *or* a queen this summer. "And, Grandma, I have to tell you: I didn't get the part of queen either."

"Why? What happened?"

"Kareena cast Jenna as the lead. I didn't get any part in the show. She asked me to help with the finances. I'm okay with it, Grandma, really. Kareena's right, Jenna already looks like an African queen."

Grandma Rose removes her arm. "You can't cast someone based on how they *look*, it's how they *act* that matters. What is that girl thinking?"

"Grandma! Jenna's a brilliant actor! I'm really pretty bad. *Please* don't say anything to Kareena!"

"I promised I wasn't going to get involved, didn't I? But maybe I can give you some one-on-one acting lessons, Chantal."

Didu reclaims her sofa spot and the loose end of her white sari floats across my lap. "Shanti darling, Kathak is the main reason why I am telling you to grow your hair. They sell creams that make it soft and straight, and you can add in extensions at one of those salons—"

"I like my hair, Didu," I say quickly. I shift my hips, trying to eke out more space for myself.

Grandma Rose studies my expression. "Don't worry, honey. *I'll* talk to that dance teacher."

"I have already tried that," Didu says. "That Singh lady does not listen to sense. She is far too Americanized to teach that class."

"Maybe she couldn't understand your accent," says Grandma Rose.

"Hah! I was speaking English perfectly, wasn't I, Shanti?"

I nod. She'd made herself pretty clear.

There's a silence. I try and take a deep breath, but I'm too squeezed in the small, hot space between the grandmothers.

Didu pats my leg. "Don't worry, darling. Every eye is going to be on you at that recital. Not on that Uma girl. But are you sure you don't want to grow your hair?"

Aaaaaand . . . we're back to hair again. Didu just can't let it go. "Chantal has African hair," Grandma Rose says, throwing a look down the sofa that would have silenced anybody except Didu.

Didu leans across me to scowl at Grandma Rose. Now I can hardly breathe. Why do both grandmothers have to be so . . . voluptuous? "Only one African lives in this house," Didu says. "A child's race comes from her mother."

"Not in America," says Grandma Rose. "If you have any African blood at all, people assume you're black. And Chantal looks black. She's a beautiful black girl, something to be proud of."

The heat's coming at me from both sides. I'm surprised the sofa doesn't explode into flames. I glance at Didu's stony face. "But I'm Indian, too."

"She is indeed," says Didu. "Bengali, mind you."

"People will treat her like she's black," Grandma Rose says across me. "You better wake up to the reality of what that means in this country."

"That is exactly what I worried about when we moved here," Didu says. "If only my daughter had listened to me."

That does it. I'm tired of being talked about like I'm not here. And even worse—like I shouldn't be here. I'm sick of being yanked back and forth between old-lady hands. How did this terrible competition get started, anyway?

Just then, as if on cue, Mom and Dad enter the living room. They take one look at our faces and spin around at the same time. The move is so smooth and fast, it looks choreographed.

Elbowing the grandmothers out of my way, I leap off the couch and block my parents' escape. "It's your fault!" I yell. "It's ALL YOUR FAULT!"

My parents' eyes widen in shock, because I never yell.

Behind them, Grandma Rose snorts. Of course.

Wait for it. Yep, there's Didu's loud, loud sigh.

"*What's* our fault, Shanti?" Dad asks.

Mom doesn't say anything, so I glare at her with my hands on my hips. Ms. Sonia Das Johnson crusades for women's rights all over the planet? What about the rights of one girl, right here, under her own roof?

"YOU DON'T GET IT, DO YOU?!"

"Get what, darling?" Mom asks.

"I'm not BLACK enough for SOME people. I'm not IN-DIAN enough for OTHER people. The whole thing stinks and I wish the two of you had never gone to Paris together. WHAT WERE YOU THINKING?"

Even *I've* never seen me this angry. Shanti the Peace-maker, always having to manage the tension between two stubborn old women. Shanti the Compliant. Why did I try out for that play when I've never wanted to act? Shanti the Meek. I'm the best darn dancer in that Kathak class.

Am I ever going to push back when people try to sideline me?

"Well, honey," Mom says hesitantly. "You can let other people tell you what *they* think. Or you can decide for yourself."

For some reason this infuriates me even more, which two minutes ago I didn't think was possible. "You mean *I* have to choose if I'm *black* or *Bengali*? I have to DENY one side of me? Thanks to YOU TWO and your stupid HORMONES?"

This rant feels so good I wonder why it's taken me fifteen years to explode.

"No, honey," Dad says quickly. "You don't ever have to deny any part of you."

But Grandma Rose snorts. "It doesn't matter what she chooses. That's the way it is in America. If she looks black, people will treat her like she's black. Both the good and the bad. You're black, Chantal." It sounds like an imperial decree. Grandma Rose could play an African queen just fine.

I glare at the cards that Didu's tray scattered across the coffee table. The queen of hearts and the queen of clubs are the only two that are face up, far away from each other with the whole pack between them. My eyes blur and my throat feels tight. Who *says* they don't make a pair? Who makes *up* the stupid rules, anyway?

With a move that feels like classic Kathak, I squat and swing my hands across the surface to sweep all the cards to the floor. Then I slap my palms in three sets of three on the table, like a tabla accompaniment: "I. Am. Black," I say. "I. Am. Bengali. I. Am. BOTH."

The grandmothers are quiet. For once. The fury drains as fast as it came, and I slump cross-legged on the floor and close my eyes. I can sense the stillness around me, as if a hurricane has come and gone and everyone is assessing the damage.

Dad makes the first move. His long, gentle fingers tuck a tissue into my hand. I wipe my eyes and blow my nose. Hard. The grandmothers are leaning forward, still sitting on the sofa, trying to pick up cards, but it's tough for either of them to reach the floor. I hate seeing them struggle like that. "I'll get those, Didu," I say. "Sorry about your cards, Grandma Rose."

They smile at me, faces so full of love that for an instant, they look almost alike.

Then Grandma Rose turns to Didu. "Wish I'd gone to that dance practice," she says. "Might have made it easier for our girl if I had."

"I should have insisted that you join us," Didu answers.

Something in her tone is different. Grandma Rose has

heard it, too. With a huge effort, ignoring Dad's outstretched hand, Grandma Rose manages to heave herself to her feet. Then she offers her own hand to Didu. "Let's get some dinner, Ranee. We're all hungry, I think."

It's the first time Grandma Rose has ever used Didu's first name. I hold my breath. I don't think Mom and Dad are blinking *or* breathing.

Didu reaches up and takes Grandma Rose's hand. With a mighty tug, my black grandmother lifts my brown grandmother to her feet. Now the two of them are standing in front of me, holding hands.

"I will enjoy your chicken curry tonight, Ranee," Grandma Rose says. "I've *got* to get that recipe of yours."

Didu nods. "I shall be happy to share it, Rose. American chickens take a long time to cook, but they certainly have a good taste when they are done."

Grandma Rose snaps her fingers in front of my parents' faces. "Wake up, you two. It's dinnertime. Let's go, Chantal."

The hand-holding grandmothers lead the way into the kitchen. Mom and Dad follow, moving stiffly, like robots.

Wow.

Suddenly, it feels like anything can happen.

I'll put my math genius to work and help Kareena make this the best show in Carver School history. We're going to pack out every performance, because that African queen is going to be *heard*.

I'm going to dance so furiously at that recital that every little girl watching is going to want feet and eyes and legs and hands like mine. They're definitely going to want hair like mine, too.

Picking up the cards scattered across the floor, I place the red queen and the black queen together on top of the stack. "New rules," I say to nobody and everybody.

Anna

United Cousins of Carver School

DIDU PUTS LIPSTICK ON FOR MY FIRST DAY at Carver Independent School. I've never seen her wear makeup before. "This is a big day, Anu," she tells me. As if I didn't know. "Put on the purple salwar, the one we made during your last visit."

Unlike Takurma, my other grandmother, Didu always speaks to me in English. It's a habit that started when I was young because my only cousin on this side doesn't speak Bangla.

"As you wish, Didu," I say. But a gold-threaded salwar is not going to change how I feel about starting school in

America. Besides, I only wear Indian clothes for special occasions in Mumbai. And this is anything but special.

"Your parents are trusting me to enroll you, Anu. It's a good thing your Shanti Didi is there to help. She didn't think you should wear Indian clothes, but for your first day, I think it's the right choice. Tomorrow, you can wear jeans—"

"Of course, Didu. I trust you." Clothes are the least of my problems. I'm Indian to the core. *That's* not going to change, no matter what I wear or how American this school is.

Or how American my cousin is. "Shanti Didi," my grandmother wants me to call her. I grew up hearing Didu talking about your Shanti Didi's top marks in math. Your Shanti Didi's brilliant success in Kathak, your Shanti Didi's "lovely, easygoing nature." It doesn't help that my cousin's a good foot taller than me and has the body of a supermodel. Now I'm going to have to see her every day in her native habitat, sparkling like the bracelets and necklaces Didu gives both of us on birthdays. Chantal Johnson, American goddess. I put on the salwar—let it be a silent declaration of my Indianness.

Carver School is twelve blocks from our apartment. The doorman points us in the right direction. Didu tucks her hand in my arm, and we start walking. I can't believe this is happening. I'm starting class nine in *New York*, not Mumbai. And I have to stay here for *four years*, enrolled in the same school as Golden Girl? I'll never survive this. Never. I'm furious at my parents all over again. They're not even here to enroll me—handed that job off like a baton to Didu and leapt on the plane to Mumbai late last night.

Okay, deep breaths. I'm familiar with life here—I've spent almost every holiday in our Manhattan flat since I was small. *I am in control of this situation,* I tell myself and lift my chin higher.

But I'm not used to *school* in America. I've been studying at Mumbai Girls' Convent School since I was small. That's my native habitat. I'm sort of a pack leader there, if I do say so myself.

"Guess what, Anu? You're going to school in New York!" Ma announced about a month ago. She sounded ecstatic, like she was telling me hunger had been eliminated from the planet.

"Isn't that GREAT?!" Baba's not an actor. His big smile was faker than the Ralph Lauren clothes they sell in Mumbai's street markets.

Oh, how I protested. I deployed all of my well-honed forensic skills. I didn't win the hard-earned title of number-one debater in Mumbai's school tournaments by accepting defeat easily. "Why is life better in a Western country? India's a perfectly lovely country. I don't understand why *your* parents chose to leave in the first place. *Dozens* of languages and different religions living and working together in an open democracy, a *booming* economy (I'm not a banker's daughter for nothing), and movies that are *loved* everywhere in the world *except* the West. You couldn't land roles in New York, Ma, but you're a *star* here."

I call my parents "Ma" and "Baba," Bengali-style. Shanti calls hers "Dad" and "Mom." I think she speaks about ten words in Bangla. Her loss.

"Your father and I are Americans, Anu," Ma said. "And so are you. You won't go to college in India, so you might as well get used to the American education system now."

Technically, I couldn't argue with that. Our passports are American. "Apart from my citizenship, *which I didn't get to choose*, how am I American?" I asked. "All my ancestors are Bengali. The two of you are Bengali."

I may be *more* Bengali than my parents, actually. I'm fluent in Bangla; they speak it like youngsters in class three. When I use English, my accent's 100 percent Mumbai. Baba's still sounds American, and Ma's shifts between Indian, British, and American, depending on which one has more power in the moment.

She uses an American accent to argue with me. "It's settled, Anu," she said, and threw big sunglasses over her eyes. Classic showbiz move.

"Besides, we want you to spend more time with Shanti," Baba added. "Neither of you have siblings. Cousins can be as close as sisters. Think of that—the two of you can be in the same school for two years."

I *am* thinking of that, but it doesn't go in the plus column for America. My life in Mumbai worked beautifully. Sunset strolls on Jehu Beach. First-class train rides. Servants to press my school uniforms and a cook to make any snack I want. My friends and family are all there—apart from Aunt Sonia, Uncle Lou, Golden Girl, and Didu, of course, who for some reason hates visiting India.

My Sen set of grandparents are a lot easier to manage than Didu. When Mom started getting more and more film gigs, they joined us in Mumbai to help take care of me. I've trained Takurdada and Takurma well; a sweet smile and polite Bangla phrases get me almost everything I need.

It's not that simple with Didu. I glance at her as we walk along. She looks nervous, too.

"Carver School is full of gifted children, Anu," she tells me. "And they're well known for athletic programs as well. Shanti plays basketball, and she's on the chess team. Not to mention she gets top marks in maths and sciences. In America, you need sports and clubs and other activities to get into a good university."

"That is good to know, Didu. But I'm trying to focus on surviving my first day of secondary school before aiming for university." Shanti, Shanti, Shanti. Maybe it's time to prove that Anu's good at a few things, too.

Didu gives me a kiss on the cheek. "Of course. But your parents are trusting me to help you."

Aunt Sonia and Shanti are waiting with Dr. Williams, the Head of School. I've no problems with my aunt, who spends her life fighting for important causes like women's rights and the end of poverty. My friends tell me that I look like Ma, but I think I have more in common with Aunt Sonia. She and Uncle Lou came over for dinner a couple of nights ago, and we talked about everything from women's rights in India to the environment to preservation of endangered tigers. It was nice spending quality time with my aunt without Shanti getting all the attention. She was at some sports camp. We haven't seen each other since I arrived.

As we walk up, my cousin comes into focus. She looks even more stunning than the last time I visited. She's tall and strong, with brilliant posture, like that statue in New York Harbor. Even her skin gleams like gold.

"Anu!" Shanti bends to give me a hug, and I feel like a small, cuddly toy. But why is she wearing those terrible baggy shorts and T-shirt? I always imagine her in spangly, sequined evening gowns with stiletto heels that make her look two meters tall.

"Good morning! I'm Dr. Williams," the principal says, offering a handshake. He looks a bit like Robert Redford, one of Ma's Hollywood favorites. "Pleasure to meet you . . . Anu? Isn't that what your cousin calls you?"

I hurry to correct him. "That's my family nickname, sir—not here, not at school. I'm Anna in public." That's another thing—my cousin doesn't even know that Bengali nicknames are only for family.

"I could get used to being called 'sir,'" Dr. Williams says, smiling. "Your accent sounds like your grandmother's!"

No, it doesn't, I think. *Didu grew up in a village in Bengal. I grew up in urban Mumbai. Our accents are utterly different.*

Aunt Sonia is peering at Didu's face. "Ma? Is that *lipstick*?"

"Shall we get started with enrollment?" Didu asks Dr. Williams, ignoring my aunt. "The first bell will ring in half an hour, correct?"

"No worries," Dr. Williams says. "All *you* need to do, Mrs. Das, is sign right here. Chantal and her mother have taken care of Anna's schedule."

"That's all?" Didu asks. "But *I* am her legal guardian while she's here, correct? Did her parents make that clear?"

Dr. Williams glances from our grandmother to my aunt.

"Of course you are, Ma," Aunt Sonia says. "But Shanti and I know the system at this school, so Starry asked us to pick her classes."

Didu picks up the pen, shaking her head. "Rose Johnson is a teacher here," she informs Dr. Williams, as if he doesn't know the school employs Shanti's other grandmother. Her words sound rehearsed to me. "She told me about the debate team. Anna is a superb debater. You'll be glad to have her."

Dr. Williams flashes his charming smile. "Sounds wonderful, but she'll have to try out. Play any sports, Anna?"

Not really, but I can't say no with Superstar Shanti standing right here. "Badminton. And a bit of cricket. That's India's national sport, sir."

"Oh, that's right, it is, isn't it? We don't offer those here, unfortunately, but I'm sure you'll find your niche. Your cousin's quite the athlete."

I know. Oh, how I know.

"May I give my cousin a quick tour before the bell, Dr. Williams?" Shanti asks. "We both have P.E. first period, so I'll get her there on time."

P.E.? Oh, I remember now. Physical Education, a requirement here in America, the land of athletic achievement. That comes *first*? Wonderful.

"Of course, of course. We're delighted to have another

member of your outstanding family with us, Mrs. Das. And now I'm off to a quick faculty meeting."

"I shall return for the debate tryout," Didu says, detaining him. "And do you have a Fashion-Design Club? Anna is quite a skilled seamstress. She designed and sewed what she's wearing right now. But that's not all—she makes Western clothes as well, and they are originals, not copies."

Dr. Williams stops at the door and takes a moment to study the embroidery detail on my salwar and the perfectly pleated orna draped across my shoulder. Auntie Sonia and Shanti are looking at my outfit closely, too.

"Wow!" says my aunt. "You made that? She must have inherited those skills from you, Ma!"

"It's beautiful," says Dr. Williams, glancing at his watch. "But I'm sorry, Carver doesn't offer that kind of training. Not too many of our students choose a vocational-technical route after graduation. But you're welcome to start a club if you can find a faculty sponsor. And now I'm off. Welcome again to Carver, Anna. Goodbye, all."

Shanti leads the way out of his office. "Come on, we're running out of time. We'll start with the sports facilities."

"I'd like to see the new pool," Aunt Sonia says. "And then I'll walk you back to the apartment, Ma."

The school is made up of several tall brick buildings

that surround a playing field and a four-season swimming pool completely encased in glass. Sparkling blue water catches sunlight through the glass roof and walls, heating up the space inside. The air is steamy, and the space inside the glass includes flower beds full of orchids, banana trees, hibiscus flowers, and bamboo. Outside on the streets, it's a crisp autumn day in New York; inside here, it's as humid as Mumbai.

Aunt Sonia takes off a sandal and dips her toe in the deep end. "That Larsen family is over the top," she says. "Their one donation paid for this whole remodel. The plants and the air in here remind me of the British Club in Ghana."

"Martin's mother wanted it designed as a greenhouse, too," says Shanti.

"I like that kid," Aunt Sonia says. "Being a trust-fund baby hasn't seemed to spoil him much. Invite him over the next time Ma comes by, Shanti. He loves her luchi."

Didu's standing near the flowers, far away from the water.

"Maybe I can teach you how to swim, Didu," Shanti calls to her. "The pool stays open for fun when it isn't being used for training or meets. But you'd have to put on a bathing suit."

Didu doesn't answer. She's staring at the sparkling water, lost in her own thoughts.

"Your grandmother doesn't own a bathing suit, Shanti,"

Aunt Sonia says. "Can you imagine her in one of your bikinis? Leave her alone."

"She can borrow one of your one-size-fits-all old-lady bathing suits," Shanti says. "That's all you wear anyway. With a *skirt*, even."

So what? What's wrong with a bit of modesty? "At Digha Beach, Bengali women swim only in salwars and saris," I say.

"That's equally ridiculous," says Aunt Sonia, shaking the water off her foot. "Cover female skin from head to toe so men won't lust after it. What about the men? Are they completely unable to control themselves? Modesty isn't that simple, Anu." She turns to Didu. "We better get going, Ma."

They kiss us goodbye. Now it's just Golden Girl and me. The bell rings, and we leave the pool area and start down a long corridor. "I'll give you the rest of the tour later, Anu. We should head straight to P.E.," says Shanti. "I'm so glad you're at Carver. Your parents said you changed schools to get to know *me* better—I've always wanted the same thing! It's going to be wonderful to have you around more."

Oh, those terrible truth-twisters! Wait until they come for the holidays. Shanti's striding along, so thankfully she doesn't notice my lack of enthusiasm.

"Did you bring your P.E. shorts and T-shirt?" she asks.

"I picked them up last week and told Mom to give them to Didu."

"Must have gotten lost in the handoff." I pause, considering my next move. "Could you not call me 'Anu' when we're at school?"

Shanti's a little taken aback, I can tell. She's called me Anu since I was a baby. "Okay, I'll try," she says. "But we're playing softball in P.E. today. You can't play softball in a salwar."

What in the world is softball? "We'll see. I can swim in a salwar, can't I?"

We head to the playing field. Girls are emerging from one of the buildings, all wearing the same baggy shorts and T-shirts as Shanti. Plain and unflattering, if you ask me, hiding curves and figures even more than a salwar or sari. And not half as elegantly. Even my cousin doesn't look as much like a Superwoman in these clothes. More like a Superperson.

"Who's that?" a girl asks. I suddenly realize how Shanti and I must look to them—a petite Bengali girl in a salwar standing next to the school's all-American athlete.

"Chantal's cousin, can you believe it? Just got here from India."

"But she's so small, like an Indian doll!"

A doll? It's not my fault Americans are overfed from birth. In Mumbai, I wasn't the biggest girl in my class, but I wasn't the smallest, either. Here, I feel tiny.

Boys start trotting out from another building. This is . . . unexpected. I mean, I *knew* I'd be going to school with boys, but I hadn't really stopped to think about it. Maybe there's *one* silver lining to my parents' decision? Some of them are eye-catching, I notice, even though they're wearing those same hideous shorts and T-shirts. And a few of *their* eyes seem to be catching sight of me. I wonder if they see a doll or a woman.

Shanti introduces me to dozens of her classmates, and I struggle to keep the American names straight: Karen, Sarah, Jim, Peter, Ruth . . . It's not that the names are new; I watch American movies and television, even in Mumbai. But there are so many faces at once, and they're all wearing the same shorts and T-shirts. I try to remember: Karen's in charge of the Ecology Club (sounds interesting, actually), Sarah's on the basketball team with Shanti, Jim's cute (looks like Tom Cruise), Peter's his sidekick, Ruth's in charge of the Jewish Students Association . . .

"Meet my friend Martin," Shanti says.

A redhead with glasses gives me a huge grin. He's five or six centimeters shorter than my cousin, and he can't take his eyes off her. *Friend?* Maybe in her mind. It doesn't take a foreigner to see he's more interested in another title, if you ask me.

A black girl in a head scarf elbows Shanti. "First days are hard," she scolds, her African accent just as pronounced as my Indian one. "Chill, girl. I know you're excited for us to meet your cousin, but Anna doesn't have to meet the whole school in the first hour."

The bell rings again. "You're right, Jenna," says Shanti. "Here comes Coach Harper. Get in your teams, everybody. Anu—er—Anna, you can be on mine."

A muscular woman is striding toward us. She, too, is wearing the same baggy shorts and T-shirt, but she's carrying a clipboard and has a whistle around her neck. To my eyes, the accessories improve the outfit. And the shorts and T-shirt combination actually seems to suit her. Maybe it's because her biceps are covered with colorful tattoos and her white-blond hair is cut short—a perfect style for her square face.

She blows her whistle. "Team A, take the field. Team B, on the bench. Martha, you pitch for Team A, right? Who's pitching for Team B?"

"I am, Coach," says Shanti. "Oh, and this is my cousin, Anna Sen." She heads off with the rest of her teammates.

The striking-looking teacher takes stock of my salwar. "Where are your P.E. clothes?"

I can't take my eyes off her tattoos. My classmates and I listen to American music along with Bollywood tunes back in Mumbai. (Inventing rock 'n' roll may be the one thing that Western countries did right.) This woman's entire body is a museum of classic rock. When she crosses her arms, Mick Jagger of the Rolling Stones gyrates on one muscle. The face of Janis Joplin dances across the other. A ball rolls in our direction, and when she bends to scoop it up, John Lennon's face grins at me from her lower back.

"Well, Anna? I asked you a question."

"I'll wear them tomorrow, Miss," I say. "Sorry. Just arrived in New York a few days ago. Still jet-lagged, I think."

"Don't call me 'Miss.' I'm Coach Harper. Chantal's pretty much good at every sport. Which one do you play?"

"Badminton, Coach Harper." A few neighborhood friends and I used to bat around the birdie for fun after school.

A roll of the eyes from Coach. "Think you can run in that outfit? And in those shoes? I'd like to see you take a stab at softball this morning."

"Certainly," I answer. We used to run races in salwars, and I never came in last. Not first, either, of course, but somewhere in the middle.

"I'll be back with a bat," says Coach. "You're up first."

She marches off. To calm myself, I imagine her in a sari. No, that doesn't work. A dress? No, still not right. By the time she's returning with a rounded bat in her hands, I've clothed her in a black leather pantsuit, earrings shaped like harpoons, and high-heeled silver boots. I've even inked in another tattoo across the back of her wide neck. Paul McCartney? All four Beatles? Ah, well, plenty of room there for everybody.

"Get on the mound, Martha," she yells. "Go stand by the plate, Anna. Watch me—you swing like this."

She smacks the air with the bat so powerfully, the wind it creates ruffles the light cotton of my salwar. I'm glad my skull is nowhere near the arc of it. So this sport is like *baseball*. I've watched the Yankees play three or four times with my uncle Lou.

I plant my sandals beside the white square on the dirt and lift the bat in the air, trying to imitate the coach's stance. The problem is, I've watched the sport on television but never actually played it. I lift the heavy, rounded bat in the air. If I'm going to swing a stick of wood to thwack a round object, I'd rather it be the flatter rectangle of a cricket bat. Of course, I was never much good at that sport, either. I let out a deep exhale. I *can* run, though.

My cousin's shout comes from the bench: "Whack it,

Anna! And then run to Jenna. Martha, take it easy on her, will you?"

Shanti's friend with the head scarf smiles and waves at me. She's standing beside another white square on the dirt about twenty meters away. Martha, the bowler—er, pitcher?—rotates her arm through the air several times. I tell myself not to flinch or duck.

"HIT IT, ANU!" Shanti again, completely forgetting my instructions to call me Anna.

The ball comes at me fast, even though it's an underhand throw, different than baseball.

I flinch *and* duck. Groans from our teammates on the bench.

"Strike one!" says the coach.

I haven't even swung the bat.

Martha takes a moment to sneer before firing the hard ball again. She's obviously enjoying demolishing Shanti's cousin in front of everybody. I try to keep my eyes open this time, clutch the bat tightly, and swing hard. The bat whooshes the air around me.

"Strike two!"

More groans.

"That's Chantal's cousin," I hear someone behind me say.

"No way. She looks like a peanut."

A *peanut*? All right, all right, I'm petite. I'll admit that. But a PEANUT? These girls don't know anything yet about the power of Anna Sen. Whirling, I give them my signature stare from head to toe. I put the skinny blonde in flat white sandals, a braided coronet, and a red maxi covered with white paisleys. The maxi would be cotton, of course, sewn by village women in the Sundarbans who fiercely protect our Bengal tigers from poachers. Perfect. My other heckler is husky, so she gets a blue-and-white vertically striped dress made in Bengal, a white bandana around her black curls, and big hoop earrings. There, that takes care of them.

"Are you ready or what?" It's Cannon-Arm Martha.

I turn to face her again. The ball whizzes by so fast I don't even have a chance to swing this time.

"STRIKE THREE! SHE'S OUT!"

I drop the bat in the dirt and trudge back to the bench.

"Next time." Shanti pats my shoulder and picks up the bat. She swings once, and the ball soars into the trees.

"HOME RUN!" shouts Coach, blowing her whistle again.

Our teammates on the bench jump to their feet, cheering as my cousin lopes easily around the bases. Home run? I wish I could run home. I keep my bottom planted on the bench and fume at the injustice of my parents. They're unpacking in Mumbai even as I sweat in this P.E. class.

Somehow, I make it through the longest hour of my life. I strike out two more times. And once, when our team is out on the field, I dash from the edge of the trees where Shanti places me and race to catch the ball. It thwacks into my open glove, falls to the ground, and three of their runners score. At least I proved that a girl *can* run in sandals and a salwar.

"Do we stay unwashed all day?" I ask Jenna as we walk to the buildings. After all that running and swinging, I've worked up a sweat.

"The schedule gives us time to shower before second period," she says. "I don't usually take one myself, but everybody else does."

We enter the locker room. It's a large, open space, full of hard metal, glass, and tiles. I look around for an area to undress. To my dismay, this blindingly white arena has not one hidden corner for privacy. Showerheads line one wall, with see-through plastic curtains between them. Lockers, benches, mirrors—even *privies,* separated only by low walls—leave all of us in full sight.

To my complete shock, my cousin and the rest of her classmates start taking off their clothes right in front of each other. In public. *All* of their clothes. Shorts, shirts, bras, and underwear.

Everyone, that is, except Jenna, who turns to face a wall,

lifts her T-shirt, and starts dabbing her underarms with a wet washcloth.

While my cousin and her friends shower in the open, I wait on a bench, pretending to study my class schedule. Oh. My. Goodness. I can't remember seeing a naked body in my life, let alone so many at once. After a certain age, maybe nine or so, Bengali girls are *never* seen naked by others, not even by friends. Maybe sisters, but I couldn't say for sure.

As she showers, my cousin chats with her friends as easily as if they were bundled up in winter coats. There is an untanned outline of a tiny bikini that shows up against Shanti's dark satin skin. I avert my eyes.

I hardly look at my own body in the mirror, even at home, in private. I'm way behind the curve (okay, pun intended) when it comes to developing. My chest is chapatti-flat and parts of me that should be getting hairy are still waiting for the first sign of a follicle. It hasn't been an issue back home. My popularity there is based on more substantive qualities than physical maturity.

I head to the mirrors to check my hair and salwar. The fluorescent lights expose the jet-lag circles under my eyes. Shanti comes up to stand beside me. There's still not a stitch in sight, and the harsh light illuminates her body from head to toe. "Not showering, Anu?" she asks.

"I didn't bring any clothes with me," I say.

"I'll get dressed in a minute," she tells me. "And then I'll walk you to math. Ms. Nakamura is one of my favorites. How'd you like P.E.?"

"I'm dropping it," I tell her, keeping my gaze away from her reflection. "I hate sports."

"You can't," she says. "It's a requirement at Carver. Besides, you're a decent runner."

"It's not just the sports." I lower my voice. "It's this *space*. I can't change in here."

"It *is* pretty ugly," she admits. "We were hoping the Larsen grant would cover a new girls' locker room, but Martin never comes in here. Maybe I should let him know how hideous it is."

Jenna, fully dressed, has joined us at the mirror to put on mascara. "Look around, Chantal. There's absolutely no *privacy* in here. I've hated it from day one."

Shanti still looks confused. "Privacy? It's girls-only in here. Why do we need privacy?"

Jenna and I exchange looks in the mirror.

"Not everybody in the world feels comfortable being naked in front of other people," Jenna says.

"Really?" Shanti's face scrunches up as she thinks about Jenna's words. "You're right. There isn't any place to change in private. I didn't know you've been feeling like that, Jenna. Let me talk to Coach Harper."

"I'll come with you," Jenna says. "I know you're her favorite, but I should have said something a long time ago."

"I'm coming, too," I say quickly.

"Okay, all three of us will talk to Coach," my cousin says. "I'll set up the meeting."

Jenna hands me a clean washcloth. "Here, Anna. Get this damp and dab your sweaty parts. And tomorrow, you can dress in the girls' bathroom by the front office. I did that before I learned the big-towel change. Watch me for a few days; you'll be good at it soon, I promise."

September becomes October, and the school year in America moves on. But I still don't feel comfortable here.

It's not the classes—I like that Carver teachers want students to discuss and argue in class. That wasn't encouraged in Mumbai. Math, English, physics, civics? My hand goes up first in every class so I can stir up a good debate. It's amazing what you can find to argue about when it comes to algebra.

It's not my social life, either. I join the Ecology Club, and Sarah asks me to talk about endangered tigers at our next meeting. Shanti, Martin, Jenna, and their friends make room for me at their table of juniors in the cafeteria every day.

All in all, most of my life at Carver is not as miserable as I'd imagined.

Except for P.E., and that terrible locker room.

That morning hour remains miserable. I can't catch. I can't throw. I can't hit. I swim, but with my head out of the water. All I can really do is run, but Coach Harper says I'm not fast enough for the track team. I come to school in the mornings wearing those ugly shorts and T-shirt and then race to the girls' room to change before math. I put on powder and deodorant galore, but I still make excuses to keep my distance from good-looking boys. Jim keeps inviting me to sit with him and Peter and other freshmen at lunch. But for the first time in my life, I'm too self-conscious to say yes.

Shanti, true to her word, scheduled a meeting with Coach Harper. She came with us but didn't say much. Jenna asked if the school could set up a changing space for girls who need privacy, but Coach refused. "It's 1999, and we're in America, not India or Somalia. Women's bodies are beautiful, and I never want Carver girls to be ashamed of them."

"Carver School should be a safe place for girls from every culture, Miss—Coach Harper," I argued.

But those biceps flexed, and she didn't budge. After about ten minutes, she blew her whistle and dismissed us.

Next, Jenna and I approached Dr. Williams. He listened to our petition for privacy, and then sighed. "I hear you," he said. "But the girls' locker room is Coach Harper's domain. I have to choose which hill to die on." That was headmaster-speak for *The Torture Chamber will stay as is*. Which meant Jenna and I and any other girls who might want privacy are out of luck.

And then he doled out more bad news. "I'm glad you came in, Anna. I've been meaning to tell you that you didn't make the debate team this year. I'm sorry. The debate coach says you have talent but that your techniques and approach are just . . . well, a little *unusual* and may not be successful in American-style debating. He wants to train you and a few other freshmen for a year or so."

I tell Didu the news about the debate team, and she's furious. She wants to storm the school, but I talk her out of it. I don't mind learning new forensic skills from the coach. But I don't see why I can't do that *and* compete at the same time. I have more experience than half the seniors on the squad. Still, I'm looking forward to learning from the Carver squad. New skills to deploy on my parents in our next face-to-face confrontation. Which is coming up: they'll be here for the Christmas holidays. In the meantime, I can debate in class.

Didu encourages me to launch an after-school Fashion-Design Club, but I can't find a faculty member at Carver to sponsor it because none of my teachers can thread a needle.

"Sewing is an important art," Didu rants one night after school. She drops a luchi forcefully onto a plate next to the stove, as if reinforcing her point. "Why is it less important than painting? Or sculpting?"

This time I can't keep her from visiting the principal's office. Didu and I make our case, but Dr. Williams doesn't budge. Without a faculty sponsor, there's no chance of starting a club, he tells us. Another glance at his watch, another dismissal, and Didu and I are out in the hall.

"You are a full-tuition student in this school," Didu says, glowering at the office door.

"That shouldn't matter, Didu," I say. Shanti's on a full scholarship, and she has a lot of clout around here. "Hey, wait a minute! Shanti's other grandmother! Why don't we ask Mrs. Johnson to sponsor my club?"

Didu beams. "That's a marvelous idea! If Rose can't sew, I'll teach her! I'll invite their whole family to dinner this weekend. Rose loves my chicken curry. Dr. Williams will *have* to change his mind if she agrees! That man doesn't like to say yes to new things, does he?"

"Not everybody likes change," I say. *Not me, that's for sure.*

"If you don't say yes to change, Anu, life starts to leave you behind. Now take me to the pool for a minute. If nobody's there, I want to try something."

The two of us stroll through the small garden beside the pool, enjoying the balmy air. I wander over to smell the jasmine. The flower's soft, pungent scent reminds me of home. Didu and I are the only ones here. After these long weeks of stress, I'm surprised by how at peace I feel here. I stretch out on a chaise longue near the bamboo grove and take a few deep breaths.

But then I catch sight of my grandmother, who doesn't look peaceful at all. Jaw set, arms folded across her chest, she's standing about ten yards away from the water, staring intently at it.

Suddenly, she slips off her sandals and begins to stride toward the deep end. Before I can even yell "STOP!" she reaches the edge of the pool and leaps into the water, sari and all.

There's a huge splash.

I'm frozen with shock for a second, and then leap up and

rush to the pool. Where is she? Billows of white sari are bubbling to the surface. *She can't swim!* And I can't swim that well . . . but maybe I can tow her to safety? A torrent of panic and plans crashes through my mind. I'm about to leap into the water when Didu's head breaks through the surface. She takes a big breath, and then I watch in amazement as my grandmother *swims* to the shallow end. When her feet can touch the bottom, she starts walking, pulling her sari in behind her like a fishing line. Before climbing the steps, she wraps it around herself again, and emerges with the wet cotton clinging to her curves. Her gray bun of hair is dripping but intact.

I give her my hand. "Didu! You never learned to swim. How did you *do* that?"

"I used to watch your mother and aunt in Ghana," she says. "I always wondered what it felt like, but I never wanted to take the risk. I did well, didn't I? It *is* a lovely feeling. Is there a place to dry off? We'll take a taxi back, but I don't want to drench the poor fellow's backseat. And don't tell the rest of the family about this, Anu, please? They won't understand, and I don't want to explain."

I don't understand. Please explain. Did I just dream this?
"I won't," I promise, even though I'm dying to tell Shanti that our grandmother taught herself to swim with one leap into the deep end. What a woman.

I lead Didu into the Torture Chamber, which is also empty, and hand her a towel. She dries herself off and wrings out her sari, standing in her blouse and petticoat. "This place looks like a prison," she tells me.

I haven't complained about the locker-room situation at home. Didu's already mad enough at the school. But I'm glad her eyes see it the way mine do. "I know. It's terrible."

She's narrowing her eyes and looking around. "They should fix it up. There's no privacy at all in here."

"I know, Didu," I say, shaking my head. "I know."

All five of the Johnsons show up for dinner on Sunday night— Shanti, her parents, and her grandparents. We talk and laugh and Mrs. Johnson helps herself to seconds of Didu's curry. And thirds, I notice. After serving payesh for dessert, Didu pours tea and joins us at the table. "Can you sew, Rose?" she asks.

"Not really. I can replace my husband's buttons on his shirts, though."

Shanti's grandfather pretends to faint. "Do you have a first marriage I don't know anything about, Rose?"

She punches him on the arm.

"I remember you sewing *my* buttons, Mom," Uncle Lou says, making her smile again.

"Perfect!" I say. "How would you like to sponsor a new Fashion-Design Club at Carver, Mrs. Johnson?"

"Fashion?" she asks. "I'm no good at that."

"I'll teach you, Rose," says Didu.

"I'm so busy," Mrs. Johnson says. "Kareena's graduating, I'm trying to find another apprentice, I need to cast the holiday musical . . . No, I can't do it. I'm sorry."

I push my payesh around in the dish with my spoon. Another attempt to show my skills at Carver. Another failure. Shanti's eyes are on my face. She gets up, stands behind her grandmother, and puts her arms around her.

"Please, Grandma Rose," Shanti urges. "You won't have to do much. Just sign up to be the sponsor. Didu and Anu can make costumes for your shows that will stun the audience."

Mrs. Johnson smiles at Didu. "Really? You can sew like that, Ranee? You've been hiding your talent under a bushel."

"Ma used to make outfits that were the talk of the school," Aunt Sonia says. "Starry always dressed like a cover girl."

"Why'd you stop sewing, Didu?" Shanti asks.

Didu shrugs. "Oh, I don't know. Your grandfather got a

promotion. We had a bit more money, the girls wanted ready-made clothes. Well, anyway. I've been missing it. I still have the sewing machine he bought for me."

Uncle Lou clears his throat. "Well, Mom? What do you think? Can you sponsor this club for Anu?"

"I don't have *any* extra money in my Theater Club budget," Mrs. Johnson warns. "We usually have to rummage through the storage closets and recycle old costumes. And I doubt Dr. Williams will dole anything out for new clubs this far into the school year. But I'll put my name on a form. Now give us more of that yummy rice pudding, please, Ranee."

The inaugural meeting of the Carver Fashion-Design Club takes place in the theater office after school. I put up a few posters to recruit other students, and even invite a few personally, but nobody seems interested. Even Shanti can't make our first meeting because of basketball practice. That first afternoon, only Jenna shows up to join Didu and me. The three of us sit around a small table and discuss possible projects while Mrs. Johnson flips through a pile of scripts on her desk.

"What about designing costumes for the upcoming musical?" Didu asks.

"No extra money in my budget," Mrs. Johnson says, not

looking up from her reading. She'd been right about Dr. Williams. He accepted the signed form when I submitted it, but it took him three seconds to tell me he had no money left for new clubs this year.

"New P.E. uniforms?" I suggest.

"No extra money in my budget," Mrs. Johnson says again.

It's Jenna, though, who comes up with the best idea. Ever since Coach Harper and Dr. Williams refused our request to create privacy in the Torture Chamber, she hasn't stopped steaming about it.

"Let's design and sew a privacy chamber for the locker room," she says. "You know—like a pavilion or a tent? That shouldn't cost too much, right?"

"We'll never get Harper to agree," I say, even though I love her idea.

"We'll design it, create it, and put it up without telling her," Jenna says. "I can't stand that locker room for one more semester. Besides, once she sees it, she might like it. If she doesn't, she can take it down. Nothing ventured, nothing gained."

"You're right!" I say. "Like a nonviolent protest."

"It's our last resort. Chantal's been trying to get her courage up to talk to Martin about it, but I don't think she really wants to ask him."

I had no idea my cousin was still thinking about the locker-room situation as much as Jenna and me. "I don't think she should," I say. "It's kind of demeaning—for her, to ask, and for him, to be exploited like that just because he loves her."

Jenna rolls her eyes and lowers her voice so Didu can't hear. "So you see it, too? I tried telling him to give up, but he said he's been in love with Chantal since sixth grade."

"Girls, what's the use of all this talk? Remember, I've got no extra money in my budget." Mrs. Johnson again. "You'll have to find donations if you're going to make anything."

"I shall donate material for this project to your club," Didu announces. "That locker room is downright ugly. I like the challenge of making it beautiful. But Rose, if we do this, will you get in trouble?"

Mrs. Johnson holds up a fist without looking up from her script. "The theater department brings in just as much money for the school as the athletic department. If I don't have to pay for it, I'm fine with this."

For our next meeting, a minivan taxi hauls my grandmother and five big trunks to Carver School. The custodian and the taxi driver lug the trunks to Mrs. Johnson's office. Jenna, Didu, and I are about to open the first trunk when Shanti stops by, dressed for basketball practice.

"What's all this?" she asks.

"Promise not to tell Coach?" Jenna asks.

"Of course not. Didu, what's going on? Why are your trunks here?"

"Anu's club is going to surprise the school with a locker-room makeover. And I'm donating the materials."

I open the first trunk, and light spills across the shimmering contents—piles of sequined, gold-threaded, and patterned fabric.

Shanti gasps. "Didu! These are your saris. Our grandfather gave those to you."

"I know, but I'm never wearing them again," Didu says. "Your mother took the expensive ones with her to India, Anu. But if you want, you girls can choose one or two for yourselves."

"I want," Shanti says, and starts digging through the trunks.

She's right, I think. Didu's saris are heirlooms. Most were handpicked by our grandfather, whom Shanti and I never got to meet. I, too, start looking.

"May I choose one, too, Grandmother Das?" Jenna asks, sounding a little shy.

Didu smiles. "Certainly, Jenna."

I choose a green one and a purple one, and Shanti sets

aside two for herself, one blue, one yellow. Jenna's pick is pink, to match her favorite head scarf. Meanwhile, Mrs. Johnson has been draping the rest of the material in the trunks across the table and chairs. Didu didn't just bring saris; we unpack reams of cloth (maroon, white, navy), ribbon, gold and silver thread. Shanti hoists an ancient-looking sewing machine out of another trunk. I grab a pad of paper and a pencil from Mrs. Johnson's desk and start sketching the locker room.

Over the next eight weeks, Operation Torture-Chamber Makeover becomes an obsession for the Carver Fashion-Design Club. We work after school as often as we can, cutting, sewing, and measuring. Mrs. Johnson, Jenna, and Shanti (after basketball practice) all serve as personal assistants for Didu and me. They hand us fabric, scissors, and tape measures when needed. They go back and forth to the locker room to measure. Shanti's math skills come in handy for that, and she transfers my sketch onto graph paper to make it exact. Mrs. Johnson is good with tools from her years of overseeing set design, and plans how to drape the curtains and pavilions that we're sewing. Jenna acts as security guard and cheerleader of our work in progress.

But the actual design and sewing? That's up to my grandmother and me.

It turns out that Didu and I share a lot of the same tastes, despite a fiery argument or two over color combinations.

Our club decides to execute the actual makeover during Thanksgiving break, when the school is deserted. Even the custodians get that long weekend off. The alarm system is on, but Mrs. Johnson knows the codes and has a key. She, Shanti, and Jenna meet Didu and me in the locker room on Wednesday night and the five of us work frantically for four days with a short break for Thanksgiving dinner on Thursday.

"What are you people up to?" Aunt Sonia asks suspiciously when Mrs. Johnson, Didu, Shanti, and I get up to leave right after pie.

"Oh, let them have their secret, Sonia," Uncle Lou says. "I'll wash the dishes."

By late Sunday night, the locker room is completely transformed. We look around at our handiwork, awestruck. We've gone way beyond one privacy pavilion. Suddenly, I'm nervous. "Did we go too far?"

"I don't know," Shanti answers. "It's a pretty dramatic change."

"Will Harper tear it down before the rest of the school gets to see it?" Jenna asks.

Didu smiles as she looks around. Then she pulls the

three of us into a white-sari embrace. "Don't worry, girls. We made this room beautiful, and nobody can take that away from us."

"Besides, I'll be here in the morning to handle Harper," says Mrs. Johnson.

Shanti, Jenna, and I are the first students on campus the next day, and we head straight for the locker room. The door to Harper's office is closed, but we can hear the song "Shattered" by the Rolling Stones playing inside.

Suddenly, a custodian barrels past us and flings open the Coach's door. "Someone's vandalized the girls' locker room, Miss Harper!"

The coach erupts out of her office and sprints down the hall. Shanti, Jenna, and I chase after her, and Sarah, Ruth, and a few other early-bird girls join us. Boys, too. Peter, Jim, Martin. We're all right on Coach Harper's heels when she hurtles into the locker room.

She yells a choice four-letter word, but then falls silent.

Behind us, the other students are quiet as they take in our handiwork.

Jenna steals away to press "play" on the cassette player she'd hidden in a corner, and soft music wafts through the whole room at just the right volume. The shiny, sparkling material of Didu's saris softens the walls and ceilings. The once-metallic lockers are covered with swatches of fabric, maroon, navy, white. They look kind of like an American flag, I realize. Sheer, silky saris are draped between the toilet and shower stalls, transforming each one into a private boudoir.

But the Carver Fashion-Design Club didn't stop there.

Small lamps sprinkled around the room cast cozy circles of light. (Mrs. Johnson ransacked the faculty lounge and even the admissions office over the weekend.)

Fat, sequined pillows adorn the once-hard benches, and colorful throw rugs warm the white tiles. Shanti, Jenna, and I found those at a secondhand shop in Harlem a week ago, and all three of us contributed money to pay for them.

"It's like a spa," Sarah says.

"I wish the boys' locker room looked like this," says Martin.

"Who did this?" Coach whispers.

Shanti and Jenna and I smile at each other. *Compliments of the Carver School Fashion-Design Club!* I want to shout, but we're still trying to keep a low profile.

Coach Harper, meanwhile, is standing in front of a mirror, her reflection shielded from the fluorescence by a rainbow of soft colors over her head. I look closer. Mick Jagger on her biceps has no wrinkles in the silky light. Prince looks like he's gazing at himself and likes what he sees.

The custodian taps the coach on the shoulder. "Fire code, Coach Harper. I'll have to take the whole thing down. Right now."

Shanti groans. Jenna looks tearful. I can't believe my ears. After all that designing, measuring, cutting, sewing, pinning, stapling, gluing, and Velcro-ing? We have to take it down so soon?

And then Mrs. Johnson steps forward. "You don't like it at all, Coach Harper?" she asks. "Speak the truth, please. As the good example you always are to our students."

Harper hesitates. Then: "It's not bad, Rose," she says. "I know who did it, by the way." Her eyes travel the room to find Jenna, Shanti, and me.

"Do you like it enough to let it stay, Coach Harper?" Jenna asks. "Some of it, anyway?"

"Modest women have rights, too, Coach," I can't help adding.

Harper turns back to the mirror. "It *is* more restful in here, I have to admit."

Shanti squeezes my hand, and hope rises in my heart. "Our team might perform better out there if we're more relaxed in here, Coach," my cousin says.

Harper finally cracks a smile. "I suppose I don't see anything that would make any girl ashamed of her body," she says. "On the contrary. Let's go, Rose. I'll let Dr. Williams know this is okay by me."

That's when we discover who really rules Carver Independent School—one burly P.E. teacher and one elderly drama teacher. United, they're unstoppable. With their recommendation, most of the redecorated locker room stays as we designed it, tweaked only to comply with the fire code and the janitor's needs.

Lots of good things happen after that.

Jenna and I start showering and changing in privacy. Four other girls, too, quietly thank us—and admit how awful it had been for them, pre-makeover.

Smelling like soap instead of sweat now, I get my confidence back—enough to flirt with Peter and several other boys, none of whom seem to think I look anything like a peanut.

Word spreads about our Fashion-Design Club's successful project, and a few other students sign up to join us, girls and boys.

The next time Shanti comes to spend the night, she brings her two saris with her. "I need a blouse in my size to wear with these, Anu," she says. "Maybe you and Didu can teach *me* how to sew, too?"

"I'll be happy to, Shanti Didi." It's the first time I've ever called her "older sister." "But *you* have to teach *me* how to hit a home run in softball. Deal? Ooh, I sound so American, don't I?"

"It's a deal, American Anna." And my cousin the goddess enfolds me completely in a hug, making me feel like a doll again. But the one-of-a-kind, collectible type.

Chantal

The Porsche Factor

RE-MED OR PRE-WED? ASKS A CAPTION ON Carver's social media page. The photo is a cameo of Martin and me sharing a microscope in AP Biology.

The other seniors were surprised when we started dating a couple of months ago. To tell you the truth, so was I. Martin Larsen—and *me*? Martin and I have only two things in common: science and math. We've been buddies forever, but the shift into romance during our senior year was a shock. Though Martin claims he's been secretly in love with me for years.

He invited me to junior prom last May, and when he showed up on our doorstep in a tuxedo, I was surprised by the tingle that traveled from my tiara to my stilettos. Martin had been coming over to gorge on Didu's Indian food or study for science tests for years without making me tingle. I wrote it off as the Tuxedo Effect. Martin's was tailor-made. He looked like James Bond.

Then, over the summer, he got contact lenses, and I noticed his eyes were bluer than the swimming pool his parents built for Carver School. Plus, he suddenly had a late growth spurt and grew a few inches. Now we were the same height, and those piercing blue eyes started making me tingle all the time.

One afternoon in Chess Club, after I checkmated him, he stood up, leaned over, and kissed me on the mouth.

I kissed him back. Martin's a lot kinder than Agent 007, and deep down inside, I realized his kindness has always been attractive to me.

Our classmates tease us about how smart we are: "You'll both end up being doctors or professors or something. Your kids will be geniuses." But even they call us "Harlem" and "Upper East Side" when they joke about us getting married. It's hard to miss the obvious: I'm black and Bengali, and Martin is . . . well, as white as you can get. And rich, too.

I usually change the subject when someone talks about

the future. I like Martin a lot, but there's not much hope that we'll stay together once college starts.

We're too different, and it's bound to come out one way or another.

My parents started their married life from scratch with nothing in the bank. We still live on a tight budget. Dad's a sculptor and mom's a freelance journalist; the Johnsons are about thrift stores, grocery store coupons, public transportation, and the old, black Catholic church full of people who put food stamps in the offering plate. The Larsens, on the other hand, inherited old money. They're about exclusive Manhattan clubs, invite-only charity dinners, trips to St. Croix, and the fancy Episcopalian cathedral full of powerful white people just like them.

And then there's the car.

Maybe more than anything else, it's that sleek, fast, red Porsche that makes me doubt our future together. Martin drives the ten blocks to school every day in the car he's owned since his junior year. To me it's a symbol of how my family cares about art and love and justice, while his family cares about . . . rich people stuff. Who spends that much money on a car? And wouldn't getting it as a gift wreck even the best person on earth? Martin argues that the Porsche wasn't a gift, not totally, anyway. He "bought" it from his dad. Mr. Larsen believes in hard work and no handouts and limited government intervention. He's an old-school Republican— another difference between Martin's family and mine. I'm not too political, but my parents are Democrats, and my cousin Anu is becoming so far left she can't see center.

My parents don't comment much on our friendship becoming a romance. I think they kind of like Martin, despite his family and his politics. Who doesn't? He's not stubborn or argumentative. Even though he's sort of handsome now, he's still a numbers geek who wants to be a computer scientist. He's sweet, respects my physical boundaries, and spoils me with thoughtful gifts like handing me his parents' unused tickets to the Yankees game so I can take Dad for his birthday. In fact, his entire family is known for their generosity— they donate huge chunks of money for scholarship students like me at Carver. Which means even Grandma Rose, who *I know* prays for my future yet-unknown black husband, likes the Larsens. "Martin's got no guile," she says. "I like that. And his mom never misses a Tuesday at that soup kitchen our churches run together. She's the real deal." The perfect boyfriend, right?

Except for how he coddles that Porsche.

Oh, I get that this is no ordinary car. I heard about the

day Martin's father drove it home, when it was brand-new. Mr. Larsen cared for it until the car gleamed like a jewel and purred like a well-fed tiger. Ten-year-old Martin spent hours beside his father, ready to hand over a needed tool, studying the correct way to wax, and discovering the well-crafted intricacies of a Porsche engine.

Martin tells me that sometimes he'd turn off the security alarm in their penthouse apartment, walk along the hall to the elevator, and sneak down to the garage in the middle of the night. When he was sure the coast was clear, Martin would climb carefully into the driver's seat of his dad's Porsche. Without actually touching anything, he'd pretend that he was driving, and driving fast, along the curves of an empty road.

When he was twelve years old, his father had taken him aside. *Son, if you can save the money by the time you turn sixteen, your mother and I will sell you this car.*

See? Hard work. No handouts from Mr. Larsen. He wasn't trying to rip Martin off, mind you. The sum he named was far less than what the Porsche was worth, but it was a big amount for a boy to earn and save. Martin found a janitor's job in a hotel emptying garbage cans, sweeping, and mopping. He worked after school and on weekends, and saved every penny he earned. On his sixteenth birthday, Martin proudly handed his dad a check for the required amount, and Mr. Larsen turned over the keys.

My boyfriend has taken excellent care of the car since it became his. After Martin parks the shiny Porsche in the garage of their building, his father sometimes comes down and the two of them look it over. "Good job, son," Mr. Larsen will say. "The car looks great."

And that's what worries me—if he cares so much about a car, deep down inside the two of us must be fundamentally different. Our family cares about people, not stuff. Who has a *garage* in Manhattan, anyway? Apparently, my boyfriend's family in their ultra-ritzy building. Anu's apartment, which is pretty fancy, has no garage and one doorman, but the Larsens have two doormen—one for the front door and one for the gate to the garage.

I've only heard about these father-son garage moments from Martin because I haven't spent much time with the Larsens, especially not since our relationship shifted into romance. He's been inviting me to come over, but I make up excuses. Jenna and Kareena and I, and the other scholarship kids, go to school with a lot of rich white people. Most of them are decent. But sometimes a comment slips into conversation about money or race or immigrants that isn't so nice. That kind of thinking starts with families, mostly. So I don't risk meeting any of their parents if I don't have to. Martin's never said anything like that, but he's the richest kid in the whole school. What are the odds he hasn't heard weird stuff at home? I mean, he's in high school and he owns a *Porsche,* right?

"My parents like you, Chantal," he always says. "Give them a chance."

"I know, but it's easier to study at our place, Martin," I say, and he gives in. Probably because Didu makes puffy luchi and potato curry, his favorites. Even Didu likes him. I can't help suspecting it's because he's from a "good family" with money and education, but when he comes over, I can tell she genuinely enjoys his company.

Sometimes Martin lets me drive the Porsche through the city to our apartment so I get to practice driving. I've had my license since last year, but my parents don't own a car.

One March afternoon, I get up to leave biology lab as soon as the last bell rings.

"Where you headed?" Martin asks, looking up from the petri dish he's been studying intently. End-of-school bells don't mean much to Martin when he's in the middle of an experiment.

"I have a dentist's appointment out in New Jersey."

He walks me to the curb, where it's starting to rain. "Why New Jersey?"

"No idea. For some reason, Mom sends me out to her old suburb for health care, to the same doctor and dentist who took care of her when she was a teenager."

Suddenly, Martin tosses me his car keys. "Here," he says. "I'll walk home after I finish up in the lab. You drive it to our place when you're done."

"But it's starting to rain," I say, tossing them back. "You'll get drenched. I'm used to taking the bus."

He comes closer and tucks the keys in my hand. "Drive the Porsche, Chantal."

I've driven his car in the city before but never on the highways. "Drive it all the way to New Jersey? And then back to your building?"

"Yes, of course. Just be careful. Traffic's terrible this time of day. And the rain will make things worse, especially on the turnpike."

I hesitate, fingering his leather key ring. It's stamped in gold with a golf-club insignia. "What about when I get there? Should I leave it in the garage? I can take the bus home."

Martin puts his arms around me. "Pull into our garage and ask the attendant to buzz our apartment. I'll come down and meet you. And then maybe you can stay for dinner."

"Dinner? But Martin, look at me." I pull away a bit to let him see. I'm wearing jeans, boots, and a Carver sweatshirt. My short hair's dry and stiff. Grandma Rose has been chasing me with her bottle of coconut oil all week, but I've been busy studying for exams.

Martin touches my long earrings gently, his fingers moving to trace the line of my jaw. "You look beautiful. My parents have been asking me to bring you home for weeks. No more excuses."

I suppose I can't put this off any longer. "Okay," I say, and sigh. "I'll stay for dinner."

What's the big deal, anyway? The Larsens are probably not going to be in my life forever. They're just *people*—elegant, rich, white people, yes, but they have to pee and burp just like everyone else.

Martin pulls me in again and we kiss, a gentle, sweet, deep kiss that makes my whole body respond. He steps back first. "I'll call and tell the doorman you'll be driving my car. Wait in the garage if he says I'm not back yet; I'll be home as soon as I can." He kisses my cheek, hands me his umbrella, and heads back to the lab.

The rain falls harder as I make my way to the small

parking lot reserved for faculty and staff. Most Carver students take public transportation. Except for Martin Larsen, of course. At a school fund-raising auction, his parents bid on—and won at a crazy price—a prime parking spot next to the one reserved for Dr. Williams, the headmaster.

Here it is—Martin's idol.

Red, clean, the insides smelling like . . . is that *vanilla*? I take a deep breath and start the engine. Backing out of the lot, I clutch the steering wheel tightly. It's strange not to have Martin in the passenger seat. He rarely says anything other than "Good job, Chantal," but I'm always aware of his eyes on my technique as I drive the Larsen family heirloom.

As I drive through Manhattan, I pull to a stop at the first hint of a yellow light and try not to tailgate through the stop-and-go traffic. But as I head across the river, my confidence grows and I loosen my grip on the wheel. I settle into the soft leather seat. It's kind of fun to drive alone, despite the snarl of cars slowing me down. It's so much more *comfortable* than the bus. Turning up the tunes, I take the exit to Ridgeford.

Forget public transportation. *This is the life.*

But thanks to rush-hour congestion, I'm late for my appointment. I hurtle into a spot in the dentist's parking lot and dash into the building to get my teeth cleaned.

Dr. Mitra makes small talk, asking after Mom and Aunt Tara and my grandmother. "You've got strong South Asian teeth," she says, peering into my mouth. "Good thing you inherited them from your mother's side."

I let that go. I'm getting used to bizarre comments about my biracial heritage. Most people mean well.

After my appointment, I hurry to the car. It's getting dark earlier these days, and there's bound to be some traffic heading back into the city. I don't want to be late to dinner at the Larsens', that's for sure. But when I'm about twenty feet away from Martin's car, I stop as though I've slammed into an invisible wall.

The Porsche isn't parked in the same position.

It's a good three feet farther forward from where I left it.

Did someone move it to a new spot while I was inside the dentist's office? But I have the keys! Besides, how and why would they do that? A sign that reads 10-MINUTE PARKING ONLY is now bending over the front of the car. Was that there when I parked it? I close my eyes, trying to remember, my mind racing. Maybe? Maybe not?

I stay where I am for a long minute, numb and unmoving, trying to gather my courage to move closer. *You can do this, Shanti,* I tell myself. I take four long steps and reach Martin's treasure. Oh, *crap*! The back bumper is crushed, big time. Another car must have smashed right into it!

I make myself walk around the car to the front. I can feel the sweat building between my shoulder blades. I look down. There's barely any room between the car and the wall. As it was hit, the Porsche must have lurched forward and rammed into the sign. I groan when I see the crumpled fender and an enormous dent on the front hood.

My eyes travel to the windshield wipers, where I would have left a note if I'd done this damage. But there's no note. A bump-and-run driver! Stupid, stupid person. But at least it wasn't my fault, right? Surely Martin and his father will understand? I hope it still runs, at least.

I climb into the driver's seat. But before I turn the key, I try to recall anything I might have done wrong in my mad rush to make it to my appointment on time. Suddenly, I look down at the gearshift. Oh, *double crap*! I'd left it in "neutral" instead of "park"!

If I'd put it in park, as I should have, the car wouldn't have moved. And I hadn't engaged the parking brake, either. This *is* my fault, then. Sort of. Maybe? Maybe not?

The jury's waiting for me in a luxury Manhattan apartment building, and the last thing I want to do is face Martin and his parents. I turn the key, and the car starts. At least I haven't destroyed the engine. I back out of the spot, my hands trembling, and head for the freeway. Why did this have to happen today, of all days?

It's really starting to get dark now, the rain pelting down. I drive back to Manhattan very, very slowly, ignoring the rude hand gestures of people who screech around past me. I'm clenching my jaw, and my knuckles on the steering wheel are three shades lighter than the rest of my hands. Finally, I pull into the driveway of Martin's building. The parking-garage doorman opens the gate. He doesn't look happy when he sees me at the wheel. And then he catches sight of the crushed fender and the dent on the hood. The glare he shoots me as I climb out of the car makes my stomach jump. Will Martin's father and mother look at me with the same kind of disgust? Will Martin?

My boyfriend (for now, until he sees the car) is waiting for me. He hurries toward me, shaking the rain out of his gingery curls. I love those red curls. He's drenched, of course, because I had his car and he had to walk ten blocks.

And then he catches sight of my expression. "What's wrong, Chantal? You okay?"

"Your car," I say. "Something bad happened . . . I left it in neutral, and somebody crashed into the back of it while it was parked. Some damage to the rear, and the front is wrecked. They didn't leave a note."

I wait while Martin walks around the Porsche, feeling a rush of hatred for the car. Why is this status symbol so important to rich people, anyway? It's only a pile of metal welded together with some wiring inside, destined for rust and decay. It's not *human*. Why don't these kinds of people have the right set of values? I'd like to see this machine explode into flames, like all those expensive cars in Bond movies.

When Martin comes back to join me, the droop in his posture brings tears to my eyes for the first time. He shrugs and squeezes my hand. "It's okay. Don't worry about it. Could have happened to anybody."

But I don't believe him. This is no ordinary car, as we both know so well. He may not be mad, but he's sad. He pulls me close, I nestle into his arms, and we stand quietly for a minute.

"Want me to drive you to your house?" he asks. "Mom and Dad are upstairs waiting, but I can tell them you're too upset to stay for dinner."

"No," I answer grimly, easing out of his embrace. I'm not about to let him face his parents alone with this bad news.

I'm sweating like it's the middle of summer, but I can't

peel off my Carver sweatshirt. I've just remembered that thanks to an overflowing laundry basket, I had to grab the BUSH SUCKS T-shirt Anna gave me for my birthday. Plus, I really have to pee. This is wonderful. I'm about to have an intimate dinner with the Larsens for the first time as their son's girlfriend. Not only did I trash their family heirloom, I'll need to race straight into the bathroom the moment I cross the threshold.

As we walk to the elevator, it opens, and a tall, handsome older man emerges. Mr. Larsen's gingery curls are tinged with gray. A maxi-Martin if I ever saw one.

"Dad! We were just coming up. You remember Chantal, don't you?"

He shakes my hand. "Of course. It's good to see you again, Chantal. Mrs. Larsen is waiting upstairs, but the garage attendant called and said something terrible happened to the car. Is everybody okay?"

"We're fine, Dad. The car, though—well, take a look."

Mr. Larsen heads to the Porsche and begins circling it slowly, exactly as Martin had. He flinches at the dented bumper but doesn't say anything. I hold my breath just before he reaches the front of the car.

"MARTIN!" Mr. Larsen shouts. "WHAT HAPPENED TO THE CAR?"

I try to gather my courage to answer. *Speak, Shanti, speak. Tell the truth.*

But Martin steps forward. "We had a little accident, Dad," he says. "It was parked and somebody crashed into it. They didn't leave a note."

"What an idiot," Mr. Larsen says. "I'm glad you're okay. We'll have to call the insurance company."

As the Larsen men continue to survey the damage, I wonder if I've heard right. Has Martin really said *"we"*? *I'm* responsible for the first damage ever done to this family treasure. There's no "we" about it at all. I can't let Martin take the blame for this. I have to confess.

But before I can say anything, Mrs. Larsen emerges from the elevator. Ignoring the two men in her family inspecting the Porsche, she strides over and throws her arms around me. Her embrace feels strangely familiar. Does it remind me of Martin? And then she takes my hand in both of hers and that gesture feels even more familiar. It's what my own mother always does when she wants me to know—*really* know—that she adores me.

"Chantal! Finally! We are so delighted that you and Martin . . . that is, we've always admired you, dear. Don't worry about the car. Those men and that Porsche! I think it's the way they say 'I love you' to each other. A lot easier to say the words, right? But, no. It's going to be nice to have another girl around. Come upstairs; the Thai food's getting cold."

She leads me toward the open elevator and calls over her shoulder. "Don't take too long, you two."

Upstairs, the minimalist, modern penthouse smells like sweet-and-sour soup. I excuse myself and head for the bathroom to release my pent-up pee. Taking my time, I dry the sweat from my armpits with wads of high-quality, ultra-soft toilet paper. *Martin took the blame for me*, I keep thinking. *She held my hand in both of hers.*

When I finally emerge, both of the Larsen parents are in the kitchen while Martin is setting the table in the dining room.

"Come help me, Chantal," he calls.

I join him. He's arranging china and crystal and silver on white linen placemats.

"So fancy?" I ask. "For takeout Thai?"

"My parents are so thrilled you're finally here. Mom wants to make it special."

I lean over to whisper in his ear: "I'm telling them the truth. It's not right for you to take the blame. But thanks, Martin. It meant the world to me."

"Who cares who did it? It's just a car. But we'll tell them the truth, don't worry."

I pour icy water into the crystal goblets Martin's mother has chosen for my visit. Somehow I'll earn the money to pay for the car repairs, and I'll have to break the news to my own parents, but all of that doesn't matter. Everything feels different now, thanks to an heirloom Porsche that I destroyed. My romance with Martin Larsen suddenly has all kinds of possibilities.

Anna

Off the Deep End

M Y COUSIN AND I AGREE THAT ONE OF THE smaller but stranger effects of 9/11 is how it changed our grandmother. Our neighborhood in Upper Manhattan wasn't destroyed, but the Towers were only a few miles away. Like most New Yorkers, Didu watched the footage of the attacks on the Towers for weeks and wept through most of it. But the pictures in the *Times* of those brave firefighters heading up the stairs did her in. Shanti and I have cried a lot, too—who hasn't, in New York? But Didu is *sobbing* over the photos in the newspaper.

I've never seen her like this. Judging by the look of concern on my cousin's face, Shanti hasn't either. I'm glad she's here with us. When she started at Columbia, which is only a few blocks away, my parents offered her a bedroom of her own in our apartment. Shanti heads back to Harlem for weekends and holidays, but with both of her parents working at home, she likes studying and sleeping here better.

The two of us sit quietly beside Didu, each patting one of her shoulders. I came home from school to find her at the kitchen table, reading about the day's events at Ground Zero. Her tears drop heavily onto the newspaper before her, blurring the ink. After twenty minutes or so of sitting between us in silence, Didu finally pulls herself together. She wipes away the flood of tears with her sari and then explodes into words. "Why are Americans so stupid? So trusting? They let anybody in this country! Even people who hate them!"

"I know, Didu," Shanti answers. "But that's what makes us great—the statue isn't going to put her torch down, not even after this."

I'm sad, too, but I'm not sure my cousin's right. "But what about those guys who attacked Jenna? Now she can't sleep, and I think she's losing weight."

Two weeks ago, a gang of thugs tried to pull off our Somalian friend's head scarf. Then last week, two middle-aged men actually spat on her when she was walking to NYU. Those are Americans, too, right?

"I'm trying to talk Jenna into staying home as much as she can," Shanti says. "But she loves this country, even after all that. It took her in. When you move here from a refugee camp, you see things differently, I guess."

The phone rings, and Shanti answers it. It's Martin, her ex-boyfriend, calling to check up on us. When he headed to Massachusetts for Harvard, the two of them decided to "take a break" from their relationship. *Some break.* He calls all the time. They're "just friends," Shanti says, but she hasn't found anyone at Columbia that she likes better than him. And it's been three years.

Didu and I exchange looks as Shanti fingers her hair and gives Martin an update. Update? They just talked yesterday.

"She still likes him," Didu whispers to me.

"Who doesn't?" I answer. "He's a sweetie. I don't know why they broke up."

"They are too much alike," Didu says. "Shanti needs someone with a fighting spirit."

It's weird, but she's right. Martin's a white guy from the Upper East Side with a library named after his family at Harvard; Shanti's a black girl from Harlem on a full ride at Columbia. At the core, though, they're both way too easygoing.

Didu gets up and goes over to the picture of our grandfather that hangs on the wall, which she keeps decorated with strings of fresh jasmine or marigolds. She studies it for a long time while I read the article in the *Times*. I, too, am always struck by the firefighters' bravery. These days they're digging through that rubble to hunt for traces of their comrades.

Shanti hangs up and puts an arm around Didu. "What are you telling him, Didu?" she asks, looking up at her grandfather's picture.

"I am thinking about what to do. I am thinking about what your Dadu would have wanted me to do."

Shanti peers closer at the man the two of us never knew. "My mother's such a replica of Dadu."

"You look a bit like him, too," Didu tells her. "And you have his sweet nature. Your mother didn't receive that, I'm afraid, Shanti. But Anu's mother is easygoing and sweet, just like their father used to be."

It sounds harsh, but she's right. Nobody could use the words "easygoing" or "sweet" to describe my aunt Sonia. She's feisty, and enjoys picking fights, like me. But her fight against child marriage and her advocacy to end human trafficking are changing the world. My easygoing, sweet, Bollywood-film-star mother *entertains* the world. I know whose footsteps *I'm* following. I'm applying this fall for the Fiber Science and Apparel Design program at Cornell. I just finished a draft essay about my career dream: a fair-trade company that invests in and designs eco-friendly clothes sewn and embroidered by Indian village women. Our clothes won't exploit people, destroy rain forests, or harm any animal on the planet. I'm going to make them there and bring them back here to sell to Americans. I'll probably be moving back and forth from India to America my whole life, just like my parents have. Two homes. Two countries.

Suddenly, Didu turns away from Dadu's picture. "I want to become an American citizen, girls. Will you help me?"

Shanti gasps, but doesn't hesitate a moment longer. "Definitely, Didu!" She and Aunt Sonia and Uncle Lou have been trying to convince Didu to change her citizenship for years.

I don't say anything.

"And you, Anu? Will you help me?" Didu asks me.

I can't meet her eyes. "Well . . . you'll never be able to move back to India. What if you want to one day?"

Didu shudders. "I never want to live there again. Terrible life for a widow. Besides, you girls are both here, and Sonia and Lou, and your parents will move back permanently very soon, I'm certain, Anu."

"Things have changed since you left India, Didu," I say. "It's not 1960 or 1970 there, either. Indian widows even remarry sometimes."

"Not old Bengali ones like me," Didu says.

"How do you know? You never visited us there. Not once." I can't stop the frustration from slipping into my voice.

"I still get plenty of news from the Kolkata gossip chain," Didu says, crossing her arms and ending the debate. "So, Anu, are you helping me become a citizen or not?"

Shanti throws me a look.

"I'll try," I mumble. But will I? I like having three Indian grandparents, four if you count my dead grandfather. Here in New York, or back in India, they make me feel grounded. Like a tree with long roots.

"Wait till I tell Mom," Shanti says. "She's going to faint."

Unlike my mother, Aunt Sonia has no desire to live in India again. She's a Bengali feminist Catholic wife of a Louisiana black man. "Now *that's* American," she always says.

Shanti helps Didu fill out her citizenship application and study for her oral exam. I pretend I'm busy with my studies and college applications when Didu asks me to quiz her. She gives me a look but doesn't ask again. When she passes with flying colors, I'm not surprised. She practically memorized the entire Constitution by the time the test came around. But I still have a hard time pretending to be supportive. I didn't inherit Ma's acting talent, and I'm sure Didu sees right through me.

My parents fly back from Mumbai for Didu's swearing-in ceremony, and all six of us accompany her to the New York Public Library. Glumly, I watch my grandmother and about one hundred other people from forty or so different countries line up to become citizens. We sit through an overly senti-mental video about "huddled masses" and listen to a bulky soprano belt out the words to "My Country, 'Tis of Thee."

America, America, America. Are there no other countries on the planet worth living in? The entire room begins reciting the Pledge of Allegiance in unison. I look around at smiles and tears of joy as voices in dozens of different accents declare their patriotism. Is it my imagination, or is my own family louder than everybody else? Uncle Lou and Shanti were born here, like me. We didn't choose our citizenship. But it feels strange to see the three other 100 percent Bengalis in the Das family put their hands over their hearts for the Stars and Stripes.

I don't.

I can't.

Let the rest of them go all-American—Mumbai will always feel like home to me. And Kolkata, where everyone speaks Bangla, has brown skin, knows the words to Tagore songs, and loves to eat fish. My heart is still Bengali. Isn't Didu's?

The candidates for citizenship are called to recite an oath. Didu stands with the rest of the crowd and proudly lifts her right hand. I pay attention to the words as my grandmother repeats them. What are they asking her to do?

"I hereby declare, on oath, that I absolutely and entirely renounce and abjure all allegiance and fidelity to any foreign prince, potentate, state, or sovereignty, of whom or which I have heretofore been a subject or citizen; that I will support and defend the Constitution and laws of the United States of America against all enemies, foreign and domestic; that I will bear true faith and allegiance to the same; that I will bear arms on behalf of the United States when required by the law; that I will perform noncombatant service in the Armed Forces of the United States when required by the law; that I will perform work of national importance under civilian direction when required by the law; and that I take this obligation freely, without any mental reservation or purpose of evasion; so help me God."

I don't like this. I don't like it at all. I don't like hearing my Bengali grandmother entirely "renounce and abjure" (what does "abjure" mean, anyway?) all "allegiance and fidelity" to India. I don't like hearing her promise to bear arms on behalf of America, even though there's no chance she'll ever be recruited for the Army. But what can I do? She's set her mind on becoming an American, no matter what I think.

Everybody else in the family cheers and claps when she

goes up front to receive her official papers and handshake. Afterward, we go out for a fancy vegetarian dinner in Greenwich Village. I don't even try to laugh and smile and joke with the rest of the family. To me, it doesn't feel like a celebration at all.

My parents go back to Mumbai, and life in New York starts to settle down. *Maybe nothing will change*, I think. So what if she's a citizen now? She's still the same Didu, right?

Wrong.

A week or so after the ceremony, Didu interrupts my cousin's study session. "Will you drive me to the mall, Shanti?" she asks.

"Why, Didu? Do you need something right now? Anu or I can pick it up for you later."

"I want new clothes," Didu says. "I have five hundred dollars. Do you think that's enough?"

Shanti's eyes widen a bit, but she manages to hide her surprise. "Five hundred dollars should be more than enough. Sure, I'll drop you off. Want me to stay with you?"

Didu smiles. "I still have a good eye for clothes. I know just what I want. And I have an appointment at the beauty salon, too. Besides, you have to study. Pick me up in three hours."

This is strange. This is new.

Ever since I can remember, Didu's wardrobe has consisted of six different saris in varying shades of white. I, of course, have always known why, but that's because *I* was raised in India. *That's what Bengali widows wear, Shanti*, she explained to my cousin when a younger version of Shanti asked why she didn't wear colors.

Didu's wrong, though. That's what they *used* to wear. If she'd go back to India, she'd see for herself.

On top of that, Didu *hates* it when Shanti or I spend money on clothes. She'd rather we make them at home. She's always trimmed my hair, Shanti's hair, and her own. One of her most familiar lectures is on the sin of wasteful spending. And now she wants to spend *five hundred dollars* on ready-made clothes? And then visit a *beauty salon*?

Later that afternoon, the door to my room is flung open with violent energy. I leap out of my chair and fall over a pile of books. Wild thoughts of screaming for help or dialing 911 flash through my mind.

A plump woman with short, curly black hair has broken into our home. She's wearing a flowery purple-and-white sack dress. Purple eye shadow and mascara highlight her big brown eyes. Red, red lipstick covers her mouth. The only thing I recognize is the feet, decked in a familiar pair of white old-lady shoes.

"*Didu?*" I gasp.

"Are you liking this style of hair, Anu?" she asks. "They cut it off and dyed it black. I didn't know it would be this curly."

My grandmother has always kept her long gray hair secured in a tight bun. "Uh . . . er . . ." *Breathe, Anu, breathe.*

Shanti comes in, having heard the commotion, and stands beside me to check out our grandmother. "Oh, wow! Didu, you look *gorgeous!*"

"Thank you, Shanti. Now that I have an American passport, I thought it was time to look more American. What do *you* think, Anu?"

I think you look insane. Shanti elbows me.

"It's . . . certainly different!" I manage. Am I stuck in a dream? Did I fall asleep without realizing it?

"The lady at the store told me these dresses are called 'muumuus,' and that American ladies my age wear them all the time. Do you like this one?"

She twirls so that her flowing purple dress fans out like a bell. Her movement reminds me of a Kathak dance step. The big breeze generated by her muumuu slaps against my cheeks. I must be awake.

"Totally," Shanti says. "You look *beautiful.*"

"Anu?" Didu asks.

"Yes, it's very American." It's horribly American. *What is happening to you, Didu?*

She walks to the mirror that hangs above my bureau and pats her curls. "My hair hasn't been this color since your grandfather died. It quickly turned gray after that terrible day. He always used to like my hair. And what do you think of the makeup?"

"It's STUNNING!" says my cousin. She's going to run out of synonyms pretty soon. I hope.

"Anu?" Didu asks again, frowning at me.

"The colors are nice," I say.

It's the truth, actually. To see her in all that purple *is* beautiful. She's been so muted and invisible, wearing white, white, and more white. The red lipstick and purple eye shadow that matches her muumuu somehow make her look regal, dazzling, eye-catching.

She turns back to the mirror. "Your grandfather loved to see me in a brightly colored sari."

"Why did you stop wearing them, then?" I ask. "You wouldn't have had to in Kolkata."

"That doesn't matter now," she says, shifting from one old-lady shoe to the other and eyeing her reflection. "Now I am an American woman—I can wear whatever I want!"

"Hooray!" says Shanti the cheerleader.

The next thing Didu says, though, is horrifying to both of us. "Shanti, will you teach me to drive?"

The first sighting of the new rainbow-colored, curly-haired version of Didu knocks my aunt and uncle off balance. Shanti and I meet the two of them in a café to talk it over.

"I read an article about how 9/11 especially affected elderly people," Uncle Lou says.

"Yes, that's it!" I say. "Maybe something snapped that day."

"Maybe she needs to see a counselor," Aunt Sonia says.

"Of course she does," I say.

"Maybe she needs some space to figure it out," Shanti says. "Why don't we leave her alone for a while and see what happens?"

I glare at my cousin. "I can't believe you agreed to teach her to drive. Do you really think she'll be safe out there?"

"Martin's a great teacher. He taught me, didn't he? His car's still at his parents', but he told me I can use it anytime I want. And so can Didu."

Aunt Sonia laughs. "My mother, driving a Porsche! Talk about the American dream!"

"American nightmare, you mean," I say.

"You're an American, too, Anu," Shanti tells me.

As if I didn't know. "I'm getting sick of all this in-your-face patriotism," I say. "Yes, the attacks were terrible and heartbreaking. But this country still has problems. Like being an imperialistic superpower that supports repressive governments, for instance? Or the fact that American corporations destroy rain forests and exploit cheap labor in poor countries?"

Shanti doesn't get mad too often, but I can tell I've pressed her buttons. "This is the greatest country in the world. Just ask Jenna where *she* wants to live! And did you see the crowd of people who became Americans with Didu? You don't see people lining up to be Chinese. Or even Indian. You're always so *critical*, Anu."

"Just give India a few decades to catch up," I argue. "America's had two hundred and twenty or so years of independence; India's only had about fifty."

"Besides, being critical doesn't mean Anu's not patriotic," Aunt Sonia tells Shanti. "Being critical *is* patriotic."

"Anyway, I wish you'd all be more supportive of Didu," my cousin says. "She's being brave, I think. It's hard for old people to take risks. We should be proud of her. She decided to change something about her life, and she's jumping right into the deep end."

For once, I don't argue. I flash back to my first semester

at Carver School, when Didu wanted to learn how to swim. She jumped into the deep end, sari and all—and she did it. But she hasn't gone swimming since.

Maybe Shanti's right. If we let Didu splash around for a while in the deep end of Americana, she'll figure out that it's not as great as it looks. And then, hopefully, she'll get tired of it all and turn into her old self. She'll still have an American passport, but she can go back to being a Bengali at heart.

"Didu does things with passion," I tell my cousin and aunt. "I guess I can support that."

Martin comes home for a weekend, and he and Shanti take Didu out for her first driving lesson. When they get back, my cousin and grandmother both look exhausted.

"How was it?" I ask.

"It is going to take me some time," Didu says, heading for her room.

Shanti waits until she's out of earshot. "Anu, it was awful! She sped on surface streets, drove onto the sidewalk, tail-gated, and yelled at other drivers."

"Why are you so hoarse?"

"From shrieking directions!" Shanti storms. "That she doesn't obey!"

I shrug. "You got yourself into this. Just don't let her die. And take you with her. How's Martin?"

"He left me the car keys and headed back to Massachusetts. I'm on my own for the next lesson."

"Good luck," I say. "Do it for the red, white, and blue."

Over the next few weeks, Shanti and I watch our grandmother try to "be American." Every morning she emerges from her room with hairspray holding up her curly hairstyle. Colorful muumuus cover her curves, and never the same one twice. How many of those can five hundred dollars buy? Her face doesn't even look the same, with all that mascara, lipstick, and eye shadow. I find myself wondering, *What's next?*

The answer comes in the form of two words I never thought I'd hear my grandmother use: "slumber party."

"I have always wanted to know what you did at those sleepover gatherings of yours," Didu confesses to Shanti one afternoon. "Do you think we could have another slumber party, and I could stay all night with your friends?"

My cousin looks up from her textbook. "I haven't had a slumber party in years, Didu. They're kind of dumb anyway. You didn't miss a thing, believe me. Besides, all my friends are in college now. But Anu's still at Carver . . . maybe she can host one."

I'm munching tortilla chips and reading the newspaper. "Sorry. We never had 'slumber parties' in Mumbai. Indian kids usually don't spend the night at other people's houses unless they're family. I wouldn't know what to do."

Shanti goes back to studying computer science. Didu leaves the room without a word but I catch her wistful expression. A *slumber party*? That's "becoming American"? But maybe it *is* a rite of passage around here. What do I know? At least it sounds harmless. "Can't you host a slumber party for her?" I ask Shanti, even though I'm not sure why I'm helping Didu. Maybe taking care of the elderly is ingrained in my Indian genes. "You could use a night off anyway. You've been studying like crazy."

"I'm in college, not junior high. Besides, who would come?"

"Did you see how sad she looked when you said no? Jenna will come, for sure. And invite some of your other Carver friends. They all know Didu."

Shanti doesn't like to let Didu down, either, so she invites Kareena and Jenna to our apartment for a slumber party. They both accept the invitation on the spot.

"A sleepover?" asks Jenna. "I've always wanted to go to one of those. You stopped having them by the time I moved to America."

Kareena's crazy-busy with her theater job, but she says she'll make the time. "Teach Grandmother Das how to slumber-party? I'd love to."

On the night of the sleepover, she and Shanti regress easily to twelve-year-old behavior. Their "lessons" include eating massive amounts of chocolate and cheese curls. Jenna and Shanti battle Kareena and me in a massive pillow fight while Didu referees. I head to my room when they all start painting each other's toenails. At midnight, I can hear them shrieking at the creepy '80s slasher movie they rented. At two a.m., I hear Didu sneak out of her sleeping bag, tiptoe into her bedroom, and settle into her own bed with a sigh. Shanti and her guests are still asleep when she sneaks back at sunrise.

Didu's next move is much more annoying than a slumber party. She begins watching tons of television as a way to master American culture. And thanks to a talent-competition show called *American Idol*, she gets hooked on country music. She stocks up on new CDs, and now, instead of old Bengali voices singing Rabindranath Tagore songs, the baritones of musicians like Toby Keith and Trace Adkins fill our apartment.

I'm a die-hard classic rock 'n' roll fan and love Bollywood music, of course. Shanti prefers R & B and pop. But neither of us can stand country music. We put headphones on when Didu's belting out songs about red roads, barroom brawls, magnolia blossoms, and lonely cowboys.

"Do you really like all that drawling?" Shanti asks when Didu pauses for a snack.

"Country songs are giving the listener a sense of place," Didu says. "They remind me of Tagore's music."

She has a point there. Jute farms and dairy farms have something in common. And a muddy river is a muddy river, whether it's in Bengal or in Baton Rouge.

My grandmother's identity crisis is fascinating and frightening at the same time, like a slasher movie you can't stop watching. I'm mesmerized by what she chooses to adopt from American culture.

"I want to go to a Yankees game," Didu says at breakfast the next morning.

Of course. Baseball. The all-American sport.

My cousin looks at me.

You, you, you, I mouth silently.

Shanti shakes her head, accepting defeat. "Okay, Didu," she says. "I'll see if Martin can get tickets."

The evening that Shanti and Didu get ready to go to Yankee Stadium, I put on a new salwar I just finished. I'm meeting Jenna at NYU to hear a public lecture about our overheating planet. There might be a guy there with an actual opinion or two. I'm sure plenty of men in New York care about climate change—which makes them *hot* to me, pun intended—but none of them are at my school. Most guys at Carver seem more interested in making money than in improving the world. Bring on the planet-changing, passionate college men, I say.

"Have fun, Anu," Didu tells me before we part ways. She sounds excited. Not only did Martin get second-row seats, but the Yankees are playing the Red Sox. Didu's put on a blue-and-white striped muumuu for the occasion.

"Yeah. Have fun," Shanti says, and she doesn't sound excited at all.

When I get home from the lecture, I'm humming because I met a *very* passionate guy there, a freshman at NYU who's studying ecology. Shanti's in the kitchen, eating a giant bowl of cookies 'n' cream ice cream—her go-to substance in times of stress. Didu's nowhere in sight.

"How'd it go?" I ask my cousin.

"Even worse than our driving lessons, believe it or not."

"What? Why?"

"It started out okay. I bought her a program, a hot dog, even a souvenir foam baseball." She shoves a big spoon of ice cream into her mouth.

"And then?" I ask hopefully. Maybe this is the last

"becoming American" move Didu needs to make before she reverts back to her old self.

"*Everything* went wrong. She shouted at the umpires, cheered in the wrong places, and then she actually threw the foam baseball onto the playing field."

"No!"

"Yes. And it tripped a Yankee base runner. Changed the momentum of the entire game. The Red Sox ended up winning. Didu's face showed up on the big screen and the entire stadium booed."

Oh, no! "Do you think she knew they were booing her?"

"No doubt," Shanti says. "She seemed quiet on the way home. Didn't want to talk about it."

I should be glad it went so badly, I suppose, but I sigh instead. *Poor Didu!*

Shanti looks at me.

"What?" I ask.

"It's kind of creepy to hear our grandmother's exact sigh coming out of you, Anu."

The botched baseball game doesn't make a dent in Didu's mission. She wakes up cheerful after a good night's sleep and plans her next move.

I've been tolerating my grandmother's time in the deep end without saying much, but that changes on Sunday morning. I'm sipping coffee and reading the paper in my usual morning haze, still in my pajamas. The back door shuts and I hear Didu humming. Suddenly, she bursts into a full-fledged rendition of "Amazing Grace," one of the only hymns I recognize. She sings the last verse standing in the kitchen, right in my face: "When we've been there ten thousand years, bright shining as the sun, we've no less days to sing God's praise than when we'd first begun."

"Where have you been, Didu? And why are you singing that song?"

"Church, Anu," she says, clasping my hand and fanning me with a leaflet advertising a faith healing service.

Church? She went to *church*? I grab the leaflet—it's from Shanti's church in Harlem—a big, African-American, Catholic church. "You went to *church* with the Johnsons?"

"I loved it," says Didu. "This has *finally* made me feel 100 percent American. I sat with Rose and Joe, and they introduced me to their friends. Sonia, Lou, and Shanti were there, too. One of the singers in the choir sounds exactly like that handsome Ruben Studdard on *American Idol*. He is looking like him, too."

I feel queasy. I know my cousin goes to church when she

heads to Harlem for the weekend. She was confirmed while I was in India, but I've never asked her about it. I see her reading her Bible every now and then. But that's different. "Chantal" was born and baptized a Catholic. *We* were born Hindu. Of course, that doesn't seem to mean much in everyday life. My parents *say* they're Hindus, but they've never set up statues or idols at home. They don't go to temple or pray. Neither do my other grandparents. How Hindu are we, anyway?

"Why don't we have any Bengali deities around here?" I ask my grandmother. "You can worship at home."

"My statues are still packed in my trunk, Anu. I didn't set them up when I moved into your apartment."

Shanti comes home. "What's the discussion about this time?" she asks.

"Religion!" I say.

"Oh, Anu's mad because I went to church."

"Mad? Why? It's a sweet congregation. You should come with us sometime, Anu. I've always wanted to ask you, but I'm not sure what you think about religion."

What do I think about religion? Not much, actually. But Bengalis are Hindus. At least, most of them. In India, anyway. And my grandmother is an Indian Bengali. There's no way I'm letting her convert. "I'm not a fan of Christianity," I say. "Think of how the Church supported colonialism. And the Crusades. Even the Nazis said they were Christians."

"I'm Christian," Shanti says. "*I'm* not crusading, am I?"

"You certainly are. Taking Didu to church with you! What were you thinking?"

"She wants to come. If her soul wants to love Jesus, that's up to her."

Not on my watch—not *my* Didu's soul. It's time for me to drag her out of the American deep end—which apparently now includes Christianity.

I unpack Didu's suitcase of Hindu gods and goddesses and decide to display them near our grandfather's portrait, which just received a fresh string of chrysanthemums. Didu always stops there in the morning and evening to mutter things that Shanti and I can't hear, anyway. Maybe she'll talk to the statues, too. Or at least remember them. I also keep lecturing her nonstop about the flaws in Christianity, quoting Freud, Feuerbach, and Darwin, but it doesn't stop the churchgoing. Every Sunday morning, my once-Hindu grandmother swishes out of the apartment in a floral muumuu that skims across the tops of her tennis shoes. She jumps on a bus and heads to the Church of St. Charles Borromeo in Harlem to worship with Shanti and her whole family.

My aunt and uncle are surprised that she's going, but

they're agonizing more about Didu's driving than about her church attendance. Didu and Shanti and the Porsche have survived three lessons now. She'll probably get her license down the road. But who cares about a driver's license? Or even a passport? Citizenship and Didu's other weird choices about becoming American seem mundane now, compared to this one: leaving our Bengali Hinduism behind.

I try to convince Aunt Sonia to see my point of view, but she's disgustingly tolerant of Didu's leap into blind faith. After all, she made the leap herself back in high school.

"You don't inherit belief like you do religion, Anu," she tells me. "It's not a culture. People have to decide what they think for themselves. If Ma enjoys it, let her go in peace. She'll figure it out."

But I don't listen. I keep hammering away at Didu's new churchgoing habit, arguing and lecturing every chance I get. I know I sound kind of crazy, but I can't seem to stop. What's happening to my grandmother? Is she losing *everything* that makes her Bengali?

One afternoon, I bring home Zach, the bearded, Birkenstocked freshman I met at the NYU climate-change meeting. I'm hoping for hours of uninterrupted romantic political discussion, but Didu thwarts that plan. She takes over the conversation *and* my date. He's a musician, and it turns out that he grew up playing in *church*. The two of them spend the afternoon at the piano, with Zach teaching Didu a few old hymns that he learned as a kid.

I spend the whole time glowering. After my—our—visitor leaves with an apologetic smile in my direction, the words barrel out of me. "Didu! Will you quit trying to be so *Christian*? Can't you see how narrow-minded—"

"Anu," she interrupts, her voice gentle but firm. "You have talked. And talked. And talked. Try to listen now, for once. I like going to church. I have friends there—the first friends I have made for myself in this country. Why do you not come with me and meet them? Who is the narrow-minded one, Anu, who?"

For once, I can't think of anything to say. Didu waits for me to start arguing, but when I don't, she turns and leaves the room. I can hear her crooning a country church song called "Long Black Train" as I slump onto the couch in defeat.

On Didu's birthday, Mr. and Mrs. Johnson and a group of their church friends of a certain age take her out to dinner to celebrate. Uncle Lou, Aunt Sonia, and Shanti—who weren't invited—come to our apartment for Jamaican takeout. There's a lot of silence around the table. After the leftovers are stored in the fridge and the dishes washed, the four of us wander into Didu's room and spread ourselves across the floor. Aunt Sonia finds a white sari neatly folded in the back of a drawer and buries her face in it. The rest of us sit around, listening to one of Didu's old cassette tapes of Tagore songs.

Shanti blurts out, "I'm getting more and more worried. What's she going to try next?"

Aunt Sonia shakes her head. "I have no idea. I always wanted her to become an American, but if you met her today, you'd think she wasn't Bengali at all. I kind of miss my Indian mother."

Finally. They get what I've been saying all along.

Suddenly, Didu appears in her bedroom doorway. "What is this? You miss me being Indian? I thought all of you wanted me to become American. Except Anu, of course."

"Come and join us, Ma," Uncle Lou says, patting her arm-chair. "I think we need to listen to *you* for once instead of vice versa."

Didu plops in the chair and scans our semicircle of faces. She heaves a sigh. We stay silent, even me, waiting for her to speak.

"Those terrorists were so evil. When a good country like this one opens a door to foreigners only to get attacked in return, it changes you . . . I began to feel that this city is my home. It came nearer to my heart, not so distant. That's how it started, but now it's different. I am enjoying making friends my age in church—non-Bengali friends who don't know the customs that keep a widow so lonely. And it has been so good to wear bright colors again. I think your Baba would enjoy seeing me in them, don't you?" She glances at Aunt Sonia, who nods, teary-eyed. "But I do miss a few things. Perhaps I went a bit overboard."

"A bit, maybe, Ma," Aunt Sonia says, fingering the hem of Didu's muumuu. "But I'm glad you've started wearing colors again. You look like your old self and that makes me feel young again."

"None of us have to be 100 percent American," says Uncle Lou. "What does *that* mean, anyway? Hyphens, for better or worse, are everywhere now. And the good ole U.S.A. makes space for lots of identities."

Maybe he's right. Maybe "being American" means you still have room in your heart for other things. Old things. Good things.

"You were always great at bargaining, Ma," Aunt Sonia says. "Can you find some middle ground?"

"We like you being American, Didu," says Shanti. "But we like you being Indian, too."

"We'll love you no matter what," I add quickly.

Didu leans over and pulls Shanti and me into an embrace. We stay there for a minute, breathing in her familiar smells of baby powder and coconut hair oil.

"You still smell Indian," Shanti says when Didu lets us go.

"Is that good?" Didu asks.

"The best," Shanti answers.

"I have to admit I miss wearing saris," Didu says. "Muumuus are comfortable, but nothing makes you feel more beautiful than a sari."

She's right. I love how graceful they are. "Why don't you wear one to church next Sunday?" I suggest. "I have that purple one that Dadu bought you. Maybe I'll wear one of my own, from Mumbai. And join you."

Didu and I smile at each other. And then we both sigh at the same moment, sounding almost exactly alike and making Shanti laugh so hard that everybody joins in.

No Dot-Com Needed

THE TATTOOED GIRL IS WEARING SIX-INCH heels and a tight red dress that flares out from the waist. The hem of it swishes around her thighs as she *rat-a-tat*s down the wooden hallway past the open door of Ranee's apartment.

"But your page said you're 'old-fashioned,'" Darnell calls after his visitor. "Maybe we can go out to eat next time."

"Keep dreaming!" the miniskirted girl yells over her shoulder. "There won't be a next time! What kind of guy expects a girl to cook for him the first time they meet?"

"I thought we'd cook *together*," Darnell says. "*With*—not *for.*"

Ranee steps into the hall. "What kind of girl shouts at a man the first time they meet?" she demands.

The young woman ignores them both and jabs the elevator button.

"You're going to miss out," Darnell says. "I make a great chana masala."

His date rolls her eyes, strides into the elevator, and pokes the "L" button until the door closes.

Darnell shrugs, turns to his neighbor, and grins. Ranee sees herself through his eyes—an elderly Indian woman with gray-black curly hair, moving slowly in her gray-blue sari.

"Hello, Mrs. Das," he says. "What did you think of this one?"

"Maybe 'old-fashioned' refers to her fashion style," Ranee says. "I saw that dress on the magazine covers at least ten years ago."

"You like women to look modest, don't you?" Darnell asks. "Covered from neck to toe like you, Mrs. Das."

"That's not true, Darnell. I like girls to look stylish. My daughters always dressed fashionably—I made their clothes myself. Sometimes they even wore skirts as short as the dress your visitor was wearing."

"I enjoy the look of miniskirts, I won't deny it. But the

long wrap-things from India that you wear are beautiful. What are they called?"

"Saris. My husband used to love seeing me wear them. Now come quickly and eat what I've made for dinner tonight. You must be hungry."

"I am. And always ready for your fabulous cooking."

They walk down the hall together and enter her apartment. He's a good boy, this neighbor of hers. Yes, after decades in America, now that she's old, Ranee has become friends with a young man who lives in the apartment next to hers. But he's not just any young man—this one was sent by God's own hand. He checks on her daily, shops for her on wintry days, and delights in her cooking. She knows his parents, who attend her church in Harlem. She never did get her driver's license, so he even drives her to church on Sundays.

Years ago she might have been hesitant to open her door to him. After all, his ancestors are from Africa, like those of the son-in-law she used to resent so much. Now Sonia's husband, Lou, is like a son to Ranee. And this young black man has become a close friend. Almost family, which is good, since she's living alone now.

The first time she lived in Flushing was decades ago, after leaving London, when she had first settled in America with her husband and two daughters. Her girls don't understand why she moved back to a Flushing apartment instead of staying in her oldest daughter's Manhattan penthouse. But once her youngest granddaughter left for college, she wanted some privacy. A place of her own. She can afford it, thanks to her husband's life insurance. Besides, being back in Flushing somehow makes her feel closer to him.

Darnell follows her into the kitchen, sniffing the savory smells. "Luchi today? Or is it kofta curry?"

Thank God she hasn't lost her cooking skills, even though her hands aren't as steady these days. She tries to sound stern. "Why are you wasting time with a girl like that, Darnell?"

"She seemed like a perfect match online."

"I don't know why you children rely on computers and dot-coms to find something as important as a life partner. And why are you dressed in such a scruffy manner? You'll never find a good girl looking so messy."

He tucks in his shirt and straightens his tie. "I want a younger version of you, Mrs. Das. An old-fashioned girl who wants to get married. Raise a family. Grow old together. Is that too much to ask?"

Ranee gives him a searching look. "No, no, not at all." She finds herself picturing her two granddaughters. They're both single. Some people might think tall and elegant Shanti, with her African blood, *looked* right beside Darnell, but Ranee thinks there's just not enough fire in his spirit. Or in hers. *One* person in the match has to keep things spicy. *That used to be my job*, she thinks. *And it definitely kept things interesting.*

But Anu? There's enough fire in that girl's soul for two people. And there's more than enough peace in Darnell's. Could this be God's plan? Ranee takes a deep breath. "Can you come to dinner this Saturday?"

"Sure. I don't have anything going on. As you already know. You keep track of my calendar better than my smart-phone."

He's right. Ranee asks for his schedule every week so she knows which nights he needs a home-cooked meal.

"My granddaughter is returning to New York," she tells him. "Her parents are in London for one year due to my daughter's stage career, and they've sublet their Manhattan apartment. So Anu will be coming to stay with me."

"Is she the one who works for that big NGO in New Delhi?"

Ranee nods. "She got a promotion. Now she'll be at the headquarters, based right here in New York."

"She's decided to leave India? I thought she loved it there."

"Our whole family is here now. It's time she returns home for good. She'll be arriving Friday and staying with me until she finds her own apartment. I'm preparing a welcome-back feast."

Darnell is studying the photo of Anu on the dining room wall. "She's cute. I like her dimples. And those braids. Looks like you. Maybe an old-fashioned *Indian* girl is exactly what I've been looking for. A mini–Mrs. Das."

"She's barely a teenager in that picture, Darnell. She's grown up a lot since then." *And she's no old-fashioned Indian girl*, Ranee thinks.

He studies the large photo of Ranee's husband that's garlanded with fresh marigolds, and then the Johnson family photo that's hanging beside it. "Your daughter Sonia looks like Mr. Das, doesn't she? And even Chantal does, a bit."

"Maybe. My husband wasn't handsome, but he was a good man, Darnell. He loved my cooking more than you do."

"That's impossible," Darnell says, reaching for the plate of piping-hot luchi.

Ranee adjusts the necklace of golden flowers on the photo of her husband. Making sure the girls were settled and happy was everything to him. *If only you could see them now*, she tells his grave face silently. *And the granddaughters. I'm taking care of them, don't worry.* She wishes he were smiling in the photo. He had a beautiful smile, like Sonia and her Shanti.

"You miss him still?" Darnell asks softly.

"Every day," Ranee says. Then she turns away from the photo. "This dinner on Saturday is in honor of Anu's new job. Come at seven. And please, Darnell, wear something clean and neat. One of your suits."

"I'll be here," he said. "I'm ready for anything you serve up, Mrs. Das."

"Didu! You know how I despise matchmaking! I know that's what you're up to."

"Maybe you should put on American clothes, darling. You look so lovely in jeans with your slim figure. Or a miniskirt, maybe?"

As usual, Anu is wearing a salwar. "No way," she says. "These *are* American clothes. Didn't you know salwars are all the rage on the runway this season?"

Her braids are gone. But no matter how short she cuts her hair, it still curls around her high cheekbones. Long lashes make her eyes look big, even without mascara. Her bare feet arch elegantly, and the ankle bracelets she wears accentuate her graceful movements. *It's a miracle she hasn't found anyone yet*, Ranee thinks. *But she's so choosy.*

"Be kind to Darnell," Ranee urges. "Poor fellow! The girls he dates are monsters, just terrible."

"Maybe he's the monster."

"No, no, he's not at all. He has high standards. His mother told me that he's never brought a girl home to meet them. Nobody's special enough, he says."

Anu sighs. "Picky, isn't he? Okay. Let's get this over with. I'm so jet-lagged I can hardly keep my eyes open."

Ranee bustles to the kitchen, where she's been preparing Anu's favorite dishes and some of Darnell's, too. The doorbell rings, and she can hear her granddaughter opening the door. There's some murmured conversation, and then Anu comes into the kitchen.

"He brought these," she announces, handing Ranee a bouquet. "I'll put them in water if you give me a vase. They're gorgeous."

Orchids, Anu's favorite. How lovely. Did Ranee mention that to him? She might have. She can't remember.

"Well, what do you think of him?" Ranee asks.

"Fancy suit. But to tell you the truth, I'm a bit surprised."

"By what? He's handsome, good education, lovely parents. He works in his father's accounting firm."

Anu carefully arranges the orchids in the vase. "I get it: black on the outside, not on the inside."

"Anu!" Ranee exclaims, then lowers her voice. "That's not true. He and your uncle Lou have plenty in common. They even go to the same church—the one you used to visit with me, remember? He's so kind to drive me there every Sunday. All the way from Flushing to Harlem."

"Okay, okay. He is good-looking, I'll admit. And very smooth. Sort of like a younger, darker version of that movie star you used to have a crush on. Yes! That's it! This guy is a black Amitabh Bachchan!"

Ranee's cheeks feel warm. "Stop it, Anu! Take these deviled eggs out to the living room right now. Darnell is waiting there all by himself."

She follows her granddaughter out of the kitchen after a few minutes, carrying a plate of pakoras. Standing out of sight, she peeks into the room and surveys the scene hopefully.

It doesn't look good.

Anu is slouched in a chair, and Darnell is perched on the edge of the couch. Ranee spots him glancing from the photo on the dining room wall to Anu, as if to make sure she's the same person. The silence in the room is heavy, and Anu's lids look sleepy. Then Ranee notices that her granddaughter is studying his hands. Both thumbnails are chewed, but he has clean, strong fingers.

I want a man with good hands, Anu told Ranee once when her grandmother asked what in the world she was looking for in a husband. Darnell has wonderful hands, thank God. That's another thing he has in common with Lou.

The two in the living room haven't spotted Ranee. "Did you grow up in Harlem?" Anu asks him.

"Yep. My parents still live there. Mom makes dinner every Sunday night. Your grandmother's joined us a time or two. Do you like to cook?"

"I can't stand being in a kitchen."

"It's not for everybody. I made your grandmother's chana masala for dinner last night. She's a good teacher."

Anu smiles. "We know how good you are to her. Thank you."

There, that's better. Ranee clears her throat, enters the room, and places the plate of pakoras on the coffee table. "Dinner will be ready in a few minutes," she says, moving into the adjoining dining room to set the table.

"Tell me about your work, Anna," Darnell says, and his voice is warm and genuine. Oh, how Ranee loves that boy!

As you would have loved him, she tells the photo of her husband, who seems to be watching the scene gravely.

Ranee sets out the plates while listening to Anu. Her granddaughter describes the handicraft exports from the Sundarbans region, where tigers are in danger of extinction and girls are in danger of being sold for money. Anu's voice is lilting and charming, and the candlelight makes her brown eyes sparkle. The music of Rabindranath Tagore is playing softly in the background—the same love songs Ranee used to sing to her husband when they were first married. And maybe Darnell does look a bit like Amitabh. There's something in the shape of the face.

Ranee serves the biryani and vindaloo and keeps quiet. Anna's telling Darnell about tiger cubs, and poachers, and village women who work with her NGO to protect the shrinking habitat. She's a good storyteller. By the time he finishes his biryani, Darnell can't take his eyes off her. Ranee notices her granddaughter tucking loose curls behind her ears, fingering her earrings, leaning a bit closer with every story.

Ranee's been on the earth for more than seven decades. She can see what's happening.

Then it's time for after-dinner sweets. Ranee brings out milky rice pudding and pours cups of tea.

"I don't usually talk so much," Anu says, sipping her tea.

"I like listening to you," Darnell answers.

Anu holds his gaze, and Ranee can feel the intensity in their silence. She, too, keeps still.

"My parents would like hearing about your tigers," Darnell says finally. "Would you come with me to Sunday dinner next week?"

Anu smiles, and the shyness of it does make her look old-fashioned. A little like Ranee when she was young. "I'd like that," Anu answers.

"You come, too, Mrs. Das," Darnell says, turning to Ranee.

"Didu. Call me 'Didu.'"

The two young people exchange grins, as if they share an understanding about Ranee's plans. So what? She doesn't care if they do. A grandmother is much better at this sort of thing than any newfangled dot-com. After all, her own grandmothers made her match, and look how that turned out.

She smiles at the photo of her husband on the wall behind them. *All is well, dear husband. All is well.* And for a magical second, as the candlelight flickers across his face, it looks as if he's smiling back.

Acknowledgments

I'M INDEBTED TO MY AGENT, LAURA RENNERT; my editor, Grace Kendall; my parents, sisters, and sons; and my husband, who stood beside me decades ago as we made our marriage vows. On that day, as part of the ceremony, my sister recited our grandfather's carefully worded translation of Tagore's poem about bringing the distant near. It was his wedding gift to us.